REMEMBER ME THIS WAY

THE SOUND OF US BOOK 3

C.R. JANE

Remember Me This Way by C. R. Jane

Copyright © 2020 by C. R. Jane

All rights reserved.

No portion of this book may be reproduced in any form or by any electronic or mechanical means, including information storage and retrieval systems, without written permission from the author, except for the use of brief quotations in a book review, and except as permitted by U.S. copyright law.

For permissions contact:

crjaneauthor@gmail.com

This book is a work of fiction. Names, characters, businesses, places, events, locales, and incidents are either the products of the author's imagination or used in a fictitious manner. Any resemblance to actual persons, living or dead, or actual events is purely coincidental.

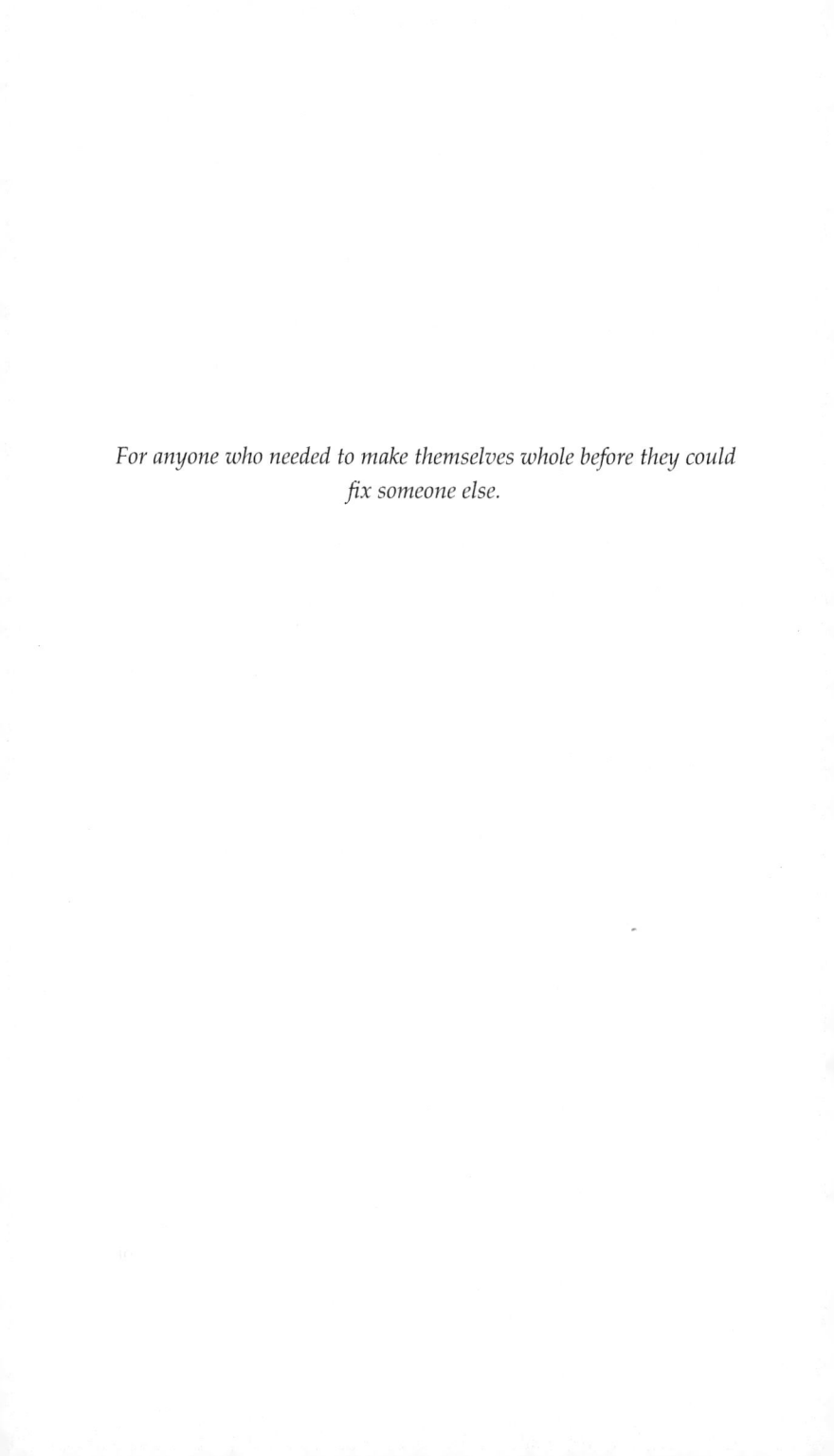

For anyone who needed to make themselves whole before they could fix someone else.

THE SOUND OF US SERIES

Remember Us This Way
Remember You This Way
Remember Me This Way

JOIN C.R. JANE'S READERS' GROUP

Stay up to date with C.R. Jane by joining her Facebook readers' group, C.R.'s Fated Realm. Ask questions, get first looks at new books/series, and have fun with other book lovers!

https://www.facebook.com/groups/C.R.FatedRealm

REMEMBER ME THIS WAY SOUNDTRACK

"Always Remember Us This Way"-
Lady Gaga

"Goodbyes-
Post Malone

"Lover"-
Taylor Swift

"Lost-
Dermot Kennedy

"Bad Liar"-
Imagine Dragons

"Rare"-
Selena Gomez

"Time"-
NF

"Happier"-
Marshmallow, Bastille

"What If I Never Get Over You"-
Lady Antebellum

"Finally//beautiful strangers"-
Halsey

"Living Proof"-
Camila Cabello

REMEMBER ME THIS WAY

The Sound of Us are supernovas in the sky and I've been following their light from the moment we met. It was easy to get wrapped in them, for me to feel like I wasn't a real person unless I was in their presence, helping them, loving them.

Since Gentry's attack we haven't been the same, and I'm afraid that the magic we had been working so hard to build may be gone forever. Addiction, jealousy, and fear fill our nights, replacing the spaces that our love used to live.

When an opportunity of a lifetime arises for me to chase my dreams, I leap at the chance to do something for myself. But it's harder than I thought to follow my own path, especially when it begins to divert from theirs.

Growing up, I never thought a happy ending was in the cards for me...but a happily ever after with the boys from the Sound of Us has been my dream since I met them.

But dreams change, and even though our love story is written across my soul, our path won't be easy.

I know their hearts though, and what's there is the same as what you can find in mine.

My name is Ariana Kent, and losing "us" is not an option.

There's no way I can save you
    'Cause I need to be saved, too
    I'm no good at goodbyes

-Post Malone, Goodbyes

PROLOGUE

It was easy to get wrapped in them, for me to feel like I wasn't a real person unless I was in their presence, helping them, loving them. They were like supernovas in the sky, and I was the lowly mortal who was blessed enough to witness their light.

And maybe that was how everything went wrong when they left, maybe I was so busy watching them that I forgot to watch myself.

Tanner had a song on their second album, a song that was #1 for six months in fact, that talked about a girl who was so above them that they were grateful just to be in her presence. He sang how he would work for eternity to be worth the dust on her feet.

It took me until now to realize that he had been singing about me. It's just that in his song, I was the guy and he was the girl.

I think that's when all our problems really began. It wasn't when I didn't come to LA, or when we didn't talk for five years, or when Gentry shot me.

It was when I realized that I couldn't survive living off of just their light.

1
NOW

ARIANA

The room was bright. Opening my eyes is the hardest thing I've ever done. But I do it, for them. For my guys.

Jensen is the first thing I see when I open my eyes. I have to close them right away, but I reopen them, seeing Jensen again. His eyes are wet, and he is smiling the widest smile. I ache to smile too. But every single movement requires great effort. "Ariana," he breathes. I try to move and grimace. I want to say more than his name, but my throat is sore. "It's okay." He squeezes my hand reassuringly.

I hear the beep of machines that remind me I'm in the hospital. I close my eyes and drift back into sleep. When I reopen them, the room is brighter and Jensen is still holding my hand. My eyes move over to Jesse, who stands directly at the foot of the bed, staring at me. Exhaustion and relief war on his face. My heart thumps hard in my chest. "Ariana." I turn my head, wincing. A woman in a white coat smiles down at me. "You're awake," she says softly. "Can you do me a favor?"

I open my mouth. "Yes." It didn't sound like my voice, but I knew it came from me.

Her smile spreads. "She speaks." She clasps her hands together. "I was going to have you cough, but you had to be an overachiever and actually speak."

A smile tugs at my own lips. I look at Jesse and Jensen. My loves. But where is Tanner? Looking around the room, he's nowhere to be seen, and I can feel my face pull into a frown even though I still feel disconnected from any real emotion. Panic hits me. Was he injured? Is he alive?

"Where's Tanner?" I croak out, and I begin to panic even more when the guys exchange somber looks. I begin to try and sit up even though the movement sends excruciating pain pulsing through my body.

Jensen and the doctor both lunge toward me in an effort to keep me laying down. I already have tears building in my eyes and great hiccupping sobs are erupting from my chest making my chest ache even more.

"Ari, he's fine. He just left for a small break," Jesse tells me frantically from the foot of my bed.

"He's really okay?" I ask. My head feels like it's stuffed with cotton, and I'm having trouble processing things at a normal speed. All I know is that I would never forgive myself if something had happened to Tanner or any of them because of my ex-husband. I can't imagine a world without them in it. Do I even have a world without them?

Apparently, I get introspective after I get shot.

I pull my hand to my chest, trying to calm my racing heart as I settle back into the hospital bed. I don't feel like I will be able to stop worrying until Tanner is in this room with me. I wince when I feel the bandages covering my torso through the hospital gown I've been put in. My body feels a little drunk, and my limbs seem heavier than I remember, but I manage to awkwardly lift the neck of my gown to peer down at the bandages.

A shadow of a memory hits me. Gentry's standing in front of me. The rabid longing in his features. The boom of the gun. And then the pain.

"Gentry?" I croak out at the guys, ignoring the doctor's attention.

There's no way that he got away. Not with all those people around.

That's why at first, I don't understand the look of shame, regret, and anger flashing across Jensen and Jesse's faces.

"He's still out there?" I confirm, the sick feeling of dread overtaking me. Am I ever going to be able to get away from him? Or is the only way away from him by death? A chill settles deep into my bones. I wrap my arms around myself shakily, ignoring the pinprick of pain from the pull of my I.V.

I shake away the morbid thoughts. My survival is a miracle that I should be celebrating right now.

Despite my pep talk, I uneasily eye the door, half expecting him to come bursting in.

I take a deep breath to settle my nerves, ignoring the wave of fatigue coursing through me. I have a lot of questions that I need to be answered before I allow a nurse to let me off into dreamland.

"Ariana," the doctor says gently, alerting me to her presence. I look at her, almost shocked to see her standing there still. I forgot about her for a second. I must be really out of it.

"My name is Dr. Rickland, and I've been helping take care of you. How are you feeling?" she asks as she puts her stethoscope over my bandaged chest.

"Tired and out of it," I tell her truthfully. "My brain just isn't quite right."

She nods sympathetically. "That's to be expected when you've been out for so long. The fuzziness should start to fade. We had to place you into a coma to help you recover after your surgeries," she explains.

"A coma? Surgeries?" I ask, thinking that I must have heard her wrong.

"Yes, you've been out for a week, Ariana," the doctor says softly.

I look at her, shocked. "That's not possible," I whisper, fingering the bandages on my chest as I stare at her, waiting for her to tell me she is joking.

"Your injuries were very serious, Ariana. You're a very lucky young woman," she tells me. I close my eyes as a tear escapes and trails down my face.

"Tell me about my surgeries," I ask, keeping my eyes closed so I don't have to see the pity on her face.

"You had two surgeries. Your left lung collapsed from where two of the bullets passed through, and another bullet was stuck in your right lung. We were able to get your left lung up and running and the other bullet out of your lung. Luckily, our lungs can heal very quickly. You aren't going to be up and running a half marathon any time soon, but you should start to feel better and better every day, now that you've woken up."

I nod, not sure what to say. I lost a week of my life. I was shot three times. It doesn't seem real. The constant throbbing of my chest makes clear to me how real it is.

"I'm going to leave you to get a little bit of rest. I'll be back in to do a more thorough check of you in an hour." She looks at the guys. "You guys should try and get some rest as well. Ariana, they haven't left your side," she says admiringly. With that comment, she begins to walk away. She stops and looks back at me over her shoulder. "I know that this all seems very overwhelming, Ariana. But it's going to be okay. The hardest part is waking up." With that bright comment, and a somewhat longing glance at Jensen that I don't particularly like, she leaves the room.

The silence feels awkward after she leaves. Both the guys look like they haven't slept, eaten, or bathed in weeks. If I didn't know that they loved me before, I certainly know it now. That unease that constantly plagues me pushes through my exhausted mind. When will enough be enough, and they get tired of all the baggage that seems to follow me everywhere?

And they still don't even know the worst thing about me.

2
NOW

ARIANA

I lock eyes with Jesse, and evidently that is all he can take. He sinks to his knees still at the foot of my bed. I reach out my hand to him, wanting to comfort him but not able to reach him. He lays his head by my feet, and I watch as his body is wracked with sobs. I've never seen Jesse cry before, and the sight of it is not one that I want to repeat.

"Jesse, it's okay," I tell him hollowly, doubting the truth of my words. How is any of this okay? How can we ever be okay again? I try to soothe him, but I'm so exhausted and weak that the words come out as more of a mumble than anything else.

"No," a voice cries brokenly from outside of the hall, and then Tanner is rushing in desperately, stopping when he sees that I'm alive and awake and for all intents and purposes, alright.

"Princess?" he asks, as if he can't believe what he's seeing is real. He looks awful. I thought that the other two looked bad, but Tanner looks like he's the one that has been in a coma for a week. He looks like he's lost at least ten pounds.

His cheeks are gaunt, and he has a pallid complexion that resembles a corpse more than a living being. But it's his eyes that scare me the most. Tanner has the most expressive eyes of the three of them. It's like seeing into his soul whenever I look into them. Right now though, they look dead, like any light inside of him has been extinguished. They're bloodshot and shadowed and pained. Tanner has evidently been battling demons while I've been asleep, and I just hope now that I'm awake he can vanquish them once and for all.

"When I saw Jesse...I thought you had...," he stutters, and I realize that he thought that I died by Jesse's reaction. Jesse has gotten himself together a bit after Tanner's reaction, but I can imagine that it looked serious from out in the hallway. I flex my fingertips in Jensen's hand, trying to get some feeling back into them. Jensen has them in an iron grip, but I don't want to ask him to let go because I can sense that he needs to be touching me.

Tanner collapses on the other side of me and reaches out a hand to touch my face before pulling it back. "I should have been here," he says in a haunted voice as he stares at me, and I look at him confused. Didn't the guys say he was just taking a break? I'm too tired to ask at the moment. It's all I can do to keep my eyes open. But it feels like if I close them so soon after waking up, then the guys might not be able to take it. I can't imagine if the roles were reversed. I would have been a mess.

"You're awake. I can't believe you're awake," Tanner is murmuring as he buries his head against my other hand that he's holding.

"Shhh," I try and whisper soothingly, trying to calm all of them down. "I'm here. I'm fine. The doctor says that I should feel better and better every day," I reassure him.

There's a song I once heard that talks about the singer not being able to save his lover because he can't even save himself. I feel like that's me in this moment. They're drowning right now, lost in the chaos that Gentry has brought to all of our lives, that I've brought to all of our lives. But I don't have the strength right now to help them through this.

I need someone to help *me* through this.

We sit in that hospital room, listening to the sound of Tanner's fears.

I've always believed that my past would prevent the future I've always dreamed of, a future where I've only ever wanted them.

Please, God . . . I pray as I haven't done in ages.

Focused and intent, I plead for our health and safety, losing myself in the constant mantra of prayer.

Please...fix us.

The days pass slowly, although my progress is impressive. Who knew that someone could be up and moving within just a few days after waking up from a coma?

I didn't.

The perk of being the girlfriend of the most famous band on the planet is that the hospital and the medical team that I've been given are the best available. All day and night they come streaming into the room; doctors, nurses, rehab specialists, counselors...they offer us their best. A week passes, and everything with my health is going well. But my personal life...

That's the complete opposite.

Most days are filled with silence between us. Jensen and Jesse never leave my side, even though I can tell their own health is deteriorating by not leaving the hospital and getting a night of sleep that doesn't happen in a chair or on a hospital cot. Tanner is in and out of the room, disappearing for hours at a time, coming back stinking of cigarettes and beer, his eyes red rimmed...his pupils blown up. I don't ask him questions about where he's been.

I'm too scared to hear the answer.

When it's finally time to leave the hospital I think that things will get better. The guys have arranged for us to fly back to LA, to Jesse's house in the hills, which is big enough to hold all of us. Jensen doesn't own a house, he just rents in between tour stops, and Tanner's condo in downtown LA isn't big enough to hold all four of us, so Jesse's house it is. The guys have promised their label to write and record a new single since their tour has been put on hold, much to the label's displeasure. Evidently, the guys told me that Clark actually fought hard for them for the record label to agree to the long hiatus. Apparently record breaking world tours aren't supposed to be put on hold for girlfriends.

As grateful as I am to have options, as I sit on the private plane that the guys borrowed from one of their movie producer friends, I'm reminded that without them, I wouldn't be able to do anything. I have to remind myself that what I have to offer them, unconditional love, is better than money, and it's something that none of them have ever really had.

But as I watch Tanner pour himself a double of scotch, even though it's nine in the morning, I can't help but wonder if unconditional love is even what they need in their lives at the moment. Looking at Jensen's gaunt face, Jesse's exhaustion, and Tanner's dead eyes...I'm not sure that love will be enough for us.

3
NOW

ARIANA

I don't know who I am anymore...or even what day it is. I haven't left Jesse's mansion since we arrived, and even though my doctors have cleared me to start living my life again, I haven't seen outside the opulent gates of Jesse's estate.

I'm watching an episode of *Housewives of Beverly Hills*, sitting in a bathrobe that has seen better days, my hair a mess, and feeling sorry for myself. The guys are upstairs working on the song they promised the record label...and it's not going well. I heard shouting and the sound of glass breaking earlier, but I leave them alone.

Just like Tanner and Jensen have been leaving me alone the past few weeks.

Jesse is the only one who's been around. It's been like ships passing in the night with the other two. I'll wake up in the middle of the night from a nightmare and find Tanner or Jensen on one side of me with Jesse on the other. They reach for me in their sleep, holding me close and giving me the comfort they can't provide me during the day. Tanner and Jensen are always gone when I wake up, though.

I hear footsteps coming down the stairs, and I look up to see who it is.

Jesse appears, a grim look on his face that tells me it wasn't just artistic differences going on up there. "How do you feel about getting out of here, pretty girl?" he asks me, and I can't tell who needs a break from reality more, me or him.

I hesitate in answering for a moment, staring at my chipped nails and thinking about the fact that I can't remember the last time I washed my hair.

Is this how I want to be? I've been given a second chance at life, and even though I've been working hard at recovery, my heart hasn't recovered at all. I remind myself in this moment that for every second I spend wasting away on this couch, Gentry is winning.

"Yes, let's do it," I tell him, trying to put some excitement into my voice. I obviously fail based on Jesse's grimace. "Do you think that the others will want to come?" I ask, for some reason feeling vulnerable as I ask.

Jesse is shaking his head before I'm even done answering the question. "I'm sure they would come if you ask, but if it's alright with you...I could use a break from them right now." There's a tightness in his voice that's not like Jesse at all.

I immediately nod and go to him, throwing my arms around him. "I'm always okay with time alone with you," I whisper, not understanding why I feel like crying. He buries his head in my neck, and we stand there for several long moments before he finally lets go. He takes a deep breath and then gives me that signature Jesse grin. "You know I think you look beautiful no matter what, but you might be more comfortable in something other than that bathrobe, pretty girl," he says to me with a wink, and I manage to crack a smile as well.

I pull at my robe, deciding that I'll throw it away after today. Get rid of temptation and all of that. "That's probably a good idea," I tell him. "Give me thirty minutes to look a little more presentable," I say, racing down the hall before he can answer. I'm suddenly desperate to get ready and feel human once again.

My bedroom is like a dream. Somehow while we were on tour, Jesse had people come in and transform it for me. Looking around at the opulence of it all, I can't believe that the girl from the trailer park has a room like this. There's gold and cream filigree wallpaper on the walls and a California king size bed with a cream comforter and what seems like a million gold pillows on it in the center of the room. The room is so big that it has a separate sitting area and a small kitchen with kitchen gadgets so sophisticated that I haven't yet figured out how to use them...just in case I don't feel like walking down the hall to one of the other two main kitchens in the house. It has a closet bigger than the entire trailer that I grew up in stuffed with clothes that are so expensive, I'm pretty sure that they should be in a museum. Gentry always made sure that I looked nice, since it was a reflection of him. His family was wealthy, extremely wealthy, but Gentry made it clear that his money was not our money, and I had only been given enough to look presentable for him and buy groceries. I hadn't had a say in how the house was decorated or anything else, Gentry's mother had done all of that with the help of her favorite designer. But this...this sort of rich was on a whole other level.

The bathroom was even more impressive. There was a large freestanding tub that was more of a hot tub than a normal bathtub, since at least six or seven people could fit into it comfortably. And yes...I imagined what it would be like if all of the guys happened to be in the tub with me at the same time.

The shower was equally impressive. Six shower heads

hung from the ceiling with even more spaced out along the side walls, so water could hit you from all sides. There were different settings you could use, there was even a foam setting just in case you felt like some fun. There were four different vanities situated around the bathroom, a place to put on makeup, and heated towel racks and floors. I didn't think that even Versailles could be as nice as my bedroom, although Jesse assured me that it was far nicer, and that he would take me to France and show it to me someday.

It hadn't slipped my notice that even though the rest of Jesse's mansion was gorgeous, magazine worthy in every way...my room was a step up. It was just another way that he went out of his way to make me feel special. I was pretty sure that I had a room waiting for me at Tanner's condo as well. It still didn't feel real that I fit right back into their lives after our time apart, despite the difference in our circumstances. That feeling of belonging reminded me that even though everything seemed so difficult right now, it was worth every hard thing we faced.

Despite the fact that showering felt like a luxury, I hurried through it now, trying to get as clean as possible so Jesse didn't have to wait for me for very long. As I turn off my shower, I can hear shouting again from down the hall, and my heart sinks. I definitely needed to hurry.

I blow dry my hair as much as possible before pulling it back into a chignon that I hope looks presentable. Concealer under my eyes followed by some bronzy eye shadow, dark brown eyeliner, and mascara make me not look as much like an extra in *Night of the Living Dead*. Some blush and bronzer across my cheeks, followed by some light pink lipgloss complete my makeup. After I slip into a midnight blue maxi dress...I scarcely recognize myself. It's been so long since I dressed up in any capacity that I had forgotten what I looked like. The scars on my chest will never go away, unless I choose to get plastic surgery, and I'm skinnier than I was before, so skinny in fact, that my breasts have gone down a whole size based on the fit of my bra...but I'm alive, and that's all that matters.

The shouting has stopped once again and when I walk out into the living room where Jesse is waiting for me, there's no sign of the other two guys. I resist the urge to ask Jesse what's going on. He'll tell me if he feels like it, and our time together doesn't need to be about that.

"Hi," I tell him, suddenly nervous for what he's going to think when he sees me. When he hears my voice, Jesse's head pops up from the game he was playing on his phone. Hunger lights up his eyes, and the way that he's looking at me makes me feel like my body could burst into flames at any minute. Apparently, my missing boob size isn't a problem, since I don't think I can ever remember Jesse looking at me this intensely before...and we've had a lot of intense moments as of late.

Confusingly, he takes a step backwards. "Let's get out of here before I drag you to this couch and end this night before it can begin," he says gruffly, looking like it's taking everything in him to hold himself back.

Jesse gestures for me to walk to the door, and I giggle when he continues to keep his distance from me. So, this is what it feels like to be normal for half a minute. I had forgotten.

There's a shiny black Escalade waiting for us out front, and Jesse's LA driver, Thomas, is waiting in front of it. Thomas opens the door for me and nods appreciatively. "It's good to see you, Ms. Ari," he tells me, and I give him a grateful smile. Although Jesse prefers to drive, he hates losing time in the LA traffic and pays Thomas to drive him around and run errands for him when he's in town. Thomas has helped to shuttle me back and forth to doctor's appointments and has definitely seen me at some of my worst moments.

Jesse slides in next to me, sitting so close that I let out

another awkward giggle for some reason. He smirks at me, his gorgeous blue eyes flashing at me delightedly, and grabs my hand, holding it tightly as the SUV takes off.

We needed this. I can already see that the haunted look that's been present in Jesse's eyes is fading just in the five minutes we've been in the car.

"Up for some good seafood?" he asks, and I nod, actually feeling hungry for the first time in what seems like forever. "I think they are doing fireworks in the next town over on the water tonight. How does that sound?" he asks. For some reason, the thought of fireworks makes me a little bit sick. But I brush that feeling aside, because I can see how excited Jesse looks at providing us with a nice night out.

"Sounds great," I tell him, holding his hand tighter. He doesn't seem to notice the sudden tension that has entered my body, and I'm grateful for that.

My eyes flicker out the window as we get to a stop light, and I find myself looking for Gentry. I know that another SUV is following us with some of the security staff that the guys have hired to watch out for us, but for some reason, I still expect to see Gentry at any minute.

"Ari," Jesse says gently, and I turn back to look at him, my lip trembling as I try not to cry. "You're safe," he tells me.

"I keep looking for him," I admit quietly. "I expect him to come crashing through the front door of the house at any minute. I expect that he'll pop in front of me at any time."

"It's only a matter of time before he's out of our lives forever. The police are after him, our private investigators are after him...there's no way that he can stay hidden forever."

"Private investigators?" I ask, hearing about this for the first time.

Jesse purses his lips. "We hired some investigators to help the police along. Even with his name on the national list, it's good to give the police some help."

I nod, wrapping my arms around myself to ward off the

sudden chill that I'm feeling. Will there actually be a day when I don't see his face in every crowd? I can only hope.

We drive along the coast for thirty minutes until we get to an elegant looking restaurant right on the beach. "Did you bring your hat and sunglasses?" I ask Jesse, only half joking. The guys can't exactly just go out in public anymore, especially in California, where everyone is constantly on the lookout for stars.

"We don't need it tonight," he says mysteriously, and my eyes widen, wondering if he rented out the whole restaurant to give us some privacy. "Only the top deck," he replies, and I realize that I asked the question out loud. I'm obviously not all the way with it yet.

Thomas pulls up to the side of the restaurant where a sharply dressed employee is waiting for us. The employee introduces himself as Isaac and then shows us up a side set of stairs that bypasses the entire restaurant and leads right to the top deck that Jesse has rented out for us. Waiting for us on the deck is a candlelit table for two that looks out onto the ocean. Isaac gets our drink order and then disappears. I lean against the railing, enjoying the mild ocean breeze. It feels so good to be out of the house. Here in this moment, I can pretend that we don't have any worries. The beach in front of the restaurant is blissfully empty, and it feels like Jesse and I are all alone in our own little bubble.

"The stars should be pretty amazing out here," he whispers in my ear as he wraps his arms around me.

"You and your stars," I tell him, leaning back against his chest and soaking in his perfect love.

"You love it," he replies, and I grin. My favorite memories with Jesse have all had stars in them. I'm hoping tonight will become another of those treasured memories.

Isaac brings us out our drink orders, and we listen to the specials. After both ordering various seafood items to share, we relax in our seats, talking and joking easily like we always used to. The food comes out, and we both ooh and ahh over how good everything is. Our laughter comes effortlessly, and we can't stop smiling at each other. This is what we needed.

Isaac comes out after we finish our entrees with special desserts that the chef prepared specially for us. "The fireworks should be starting soon," he informs us, and for some reason, I shiver after his announcement.

"Do you need a jacket?" Jesse asks, and I smile and shake my head.

"I'm good," I tell him, intent on not ruining the evening for no good reason.

Jesse picks up our desserts, as I carry our glasses of sherry, and leads us to a section of the deck that is set up as a lounge area, complete with several sofas and coffee tables. I snuggle into his arms on the couch as we eat the most delicious chocolate lava cake I've ever tried and sip our dessert wine, waiting for the fireworks to start.

BOOM!

Bile rises in my throat. BOOM! I fall off the couch when the explosion registers, my head cracking against the coffee table. Gentry and a gun. BOOM! Everyone is screaming, and all I see is red. BOOM! I'm falling away into darkness. Rolling to my knees, I press my hands against my ears and hum. I tunnel away, until the outer rim of my sight is fuzzy and a numbing blur eases my ragged nerves.

"Ariana?" Jesse cries, reaching for me and tucking me into his arms. When he does, the horizon comes into focus, as do the sparkles. Fireworks. It's just the fireworks starting. After each shot, the sky brightens by a burst of light, the simmering tails snuffed out by the darkening night. I would normally think it was beautiful, but right now, it seems like it's the most terrifying thing I've ever seen.

Jesse doesn't ask me what's wrong again, and for that, I'm grateful. I don't know what happened and haven't a clue on how to explain it. He picks me up in his arms and without a word, carries me down the stairs and out to the street. As he does, my gaze falls to more than one horrified pair of eyes of the employees and guests who stepped out to watch the fireworks or go home. They're all watching; watching perfect Jesse Carroway carry his crazy ass girlfriend to the car. I'm sure this will end up in the tabloids by tomorrow. I'd laugh, but I don't have the strength. It's a relief to get away from their judgmental stares when we finally get into the quiet confines of the SUV.

My dress is soaked. The sweet blend of burnt caramel, coffee, and vanilla roll my stomach. The sherry we had been drinking coats not only me but Jesse as well. I've made a mess of things.

Jesse doesn't say anything in the car, just holds me tight and strokes my cheek gently. We get back to the house in record time and once again, Jesse has me in his arms and is carrying me inside. "Good night. Call me if you need anything," says Thomas as we walk away. My eyes lock with his for just a second, and the side of his mouth raises just a smidge. For some reason, I take it as a reassurance, a been-there-done-that, everything-will-be-okay kind of smidge.

Jesse heads directly to the shower, and doesn't release me, even while turning the water on. Only after the streams are flowing does he set me down on the counter. I let my head fall, and it pounds. Remembering the smack against the coffee table, it makes sense. I'll need ibuprofen before bed.

"Ariana?" he whispers, running his fingers along my cheeks and neck, into my hair. "Talk to me." I nibble my lips, top and then bottom.

"I don't know what to say."

"Tell me what happened," he says, massaging my shoulders. I push against his chest and hop down when he gives me just enough space.

"Help me with this?" I turn around so he can release me from the maxi dress that I know I'm going to burn after this.

Alcohol has ruined the dress, but I'm not at all sad to see it go. Left standing in bra and panties, I find us in the mirror. Jesse's hands are spread along my stomach, the expanse of them covering my midsection—so strong. I close my eyes and lean back—he's hard and warm and comforting. "I got scared."

Turning me toward him, he nudges my chin up, and I'm forced to find his eyes. "Scared of what?"

"When Gentry first began shooting, I thought it was someone shooting off fireworks outside," I whisper, hanging my head, dejected. So stupid.

"It's not stupid. Tonight was too much too soon. I should have started just with dinner."

I'm so ridiculous. I'd bury my head in the sand if I could. As it is, the only thing I can do is burrow into one of my favorite places and let him wash the memories away. And hope he forgives me for making them.

4
THEN

ARIANA

Tanner is waiting for me outside of school and involuntary butterflies spring up inside of me when I see his handsome face. I haven't had very much alone time with him, and I'm just nervous because of that...at least that's what I tell myself.

"Hey," he says with a wide smile, but I notice that he doesn't look me right in the eyes. I run a hand through my hair self-consciously, wondering if there's something weird on my face and he just doesn't want to draw attention to it. It's just the stupid way my mind thinks sometimes.

"Do you want to hang out for a while, or do you have to go home?" he asks me, still not looking at me.

"That sounds good," I say too quickly, eliciting a little grin from Tanner's mouth that I immediately memorize.

"So, you want to hang out?" he asks, and I blush, realizing that I didn't answer his question.

"Yes, I want to hang out, Tanner," I respond softly.

His sexy little grin grows wider, and he helps me into his car, and we set off.

"Are we going to go to your house?" I ask after we've been driving for a while. I thought I remembered passing some of the landmarks from the night of the party at his house. Evidently, that's the wrong question to ask because Tanner's face darkens.

"I wouldn't ever bring you home while *they're* in town," he says angrily. There's an awkward silence after that as we continue driving.

We don't stop until we get to Mercy Lake. I had only been here once, during a small moment where Terry had decided to be clean for a while. It had been a glorious day, one highlighted by the wistfulness of a childhood past. She'd found the bottom of a bottle of vodka the next day, and that was that.

We sit in Tanner's car for a moment quietly, the uncomfortableness dissipating. My eyes don't know where to look. Was it Tanner's pretty face, Tanner's pretty car, or the prettiness of our surroundings? For someone who had been surrounded by so much ugliness in my life, it was a little overwhelming to be around the guys and all the beauty that came with them.

Finally, Tanner opens the door to his car. "Should we go sit out there?" he asks. "I have a blanket in the back of my car."

For some reason, my mind immediately goes *there*. And I can't help but wonder how many times he's used that blanket for purposes other than sitting. He's not looking at me, so I can't see his reaction.

"Sure," I tell him, "it's really nice outside." I'm not sure why I'm barely able to string a few words together around him. I'm going to eventually have to get used to talking. That is, if they're around that long. People have a way of leaving in my life.

He opens his trunk and grabs the blanket. He then surprises me by walking over to me and grabbing my hand. We walk hand-in-hand until we get to the narrow strip of beach that surrounds the lake. He spreads out the blanket and helps me to sit down before smoothly sitting down next to me. A cold breeze flows past, and I pull and tuck my knees into me, setting my chin on top of them and staring out at the rippling water. Tanner surprises me again by putting his arm around me and squishing close to me. I savor the warmth of his body.

"I can't wait to get out of here," he says suddenly, and there's resolve in his voice. In this moment, I know that he feels more strongly about that sentence than anything else that he has ever said to me before.

I connect with him on that statement. I don't think that there's anything I want more than to get away from here. Except that's not really true... Is it, a small voice inside of me reminds me.

"It will happen soon," I tell him, conviction laced in my words. I believe in them. They're magic when they're on that stage, and I can't wait until the whole world can see them.

"You actually mean that, don't you?" he asks, a little wonder in his voice at my statement.

I look at him, but he still isn't looking at me, and I huff out a breath. "Someday, everyone's gonna know your name, Tanner. Everything here will be just a distant memory, and there will only be good things ahead of you. I believe that with all of my heart," I tell him shyly.

There's another silence, but this time, it's not awkward.

"Why won't you look at me?" I finally ask.

Again, there's silence, as if he's weighing his next words. I'm suddenly afraid of what he's going to say. He turns just then, his eyes fierce, their silver depths threatening to swallow me whole. "I can't look at you, because I'm afraid that you'll see right through to my soul. When you see what's in there, you'll find out just how ugly I am inside, and you won't want anything to do with me, won't want anything to do with us."

I know Tanner has secrets. Out of the three of them, he's

the one that's most troubled and the one that holds his troubles closest to the vest. But I don't believe him that he's ugly inside. I've seen how ugly people can really be, and he's not like that, no matter what he believes.

He's still looking at me now, waiting for a response, I guess. I reach out to touch his face, he shivers when I touch him, and closes his eyes, like my touch is the best thing he's ever felt.

"Oh, Tanner, you could never be ugly to me. No matter how long it takes, I'll prove that to you," I tell him. He looks so hopeful at my comment that it takes my breath away. What secrets is this beautiful boy hiding that simple words from an almost stranger can have that effect on him? It's like he's literally dying for affection, and no one else can give it to him but me.

We don't say anything else that afternoon, we just sit there and savor this moment of temporarily being free of all the shit in our lives. It's an afternoon that I want to never forget.

It's an afternoon that I never did forget.

5
NOW

ARIANA

It's been three days since the failed dinner with Jesse, and I'm still not over it. Jesse has been trying to get me to snap out of it, but I've been having worse nightmares than ever the last few nights. Jensen almost had a heart attack the other night when I started screaming in my sleep. They've all been tiptoeing around me even more, which is only making the situation worse.

At least they've managed to finally start working together and pull a song together. None of them have spoken about what was going on, but the fact that the song isn't even close to their best work speaks volumes to where the band is right now mentally. The label seems happy with it though, and has started teasing the new single on all the band's social media sites.

I'm back to watching bad reality TV, but at least I've started getting ready again. I did in fact, throw the bathrobe away much to Jesse's pleasure.

Speaking of Jesse...my heart skips a beat and starts again with a big thump when the door to my bedroom swings open and Jesse walks in, dressed in a doctor's coat without a shirt on underneath it. My eyes widen when I see him. I've been writing in my journal while I listened to the television. It's an exercise I read about online that can sometimes help with anxiety after trauma. I'm willing to try anything at this point.

I stop mid word when I see him, though. Jensen is laying down on the couch beside me, fiddling on his phone.

"Damn," Jensen says, his eyes widening as he springs up to a sitting position. "Did I miss the memo about a costume party?" he asks.

Jesse smirks and strides over to us, grabbing Jensen's arm and hauling him to the door.

"What the hell?" Jensen says as Jesse pushes him out the door.

Backing him into the hallway, Jesse says, "You'll have to catch up with the *Real Housewives* another time. Tomorrow, at the earliest."

It's hard to keep a straight face when Jensen calls out, "Wait, we're allowed to have sex again . . ." The rest of his rant is muffled as he's locked in the hall. Jesse doesn't turn around. Resting his head on the door, he takes two deep breaths and then lifts and drops it once before rounding on me.

His eyes blur into a blue sky, rolling with emotion. The light bounces off them, stirring visions of perfection and hinting at danger. My heart races as they devour me from head to toe, taking in the simple cutoff shorts and tank top that I'm wearing that leaves little to the imagination. As he stalks forward, I rub my thighs together in anticipation, wondering what he's going to do.

Glancing at the clock on the wall behind me, he says, "You're ten minutes late for your appointment, Ms. Kent." His nostrils flare as he sexily runs a hand through his hair, stalking towards me.

"Had I known the importance of this engagement, I

wouldn't have kept you waiting," I tell him, tapping the pen I had been writing with against my lips.

"Well, now that you're here, I suppose we should carry on. Wouldn't you agree?" he peers down at me, and my mouth falls open. My stomach curls into a flutter as the prospect of him touching me becomes greater by the second. He's all mine. "Hmm, we'll have to check your throat for laryngitis, as well as a head-to-toe inspection for injuries."

I cough, barely suppressing a grin as he takes the last step towards me. Raising his hand to my forehead, he lays it there and then moves to my cheek. "No sign of fever, although you're looking a tad flushed. Are you feeling alright, or should we remove your clothes?" he asks, a devilish smirk across his perfect lips.

"Clothes?" I ask, losing all rational thought in the face of the wet dream that's standing right in front of me.

"Yes, clothes. Take them off." I stutter when I realize what he's asked.

He helps me with my shirt and shorts. My hands are shaking as I help him. I finally give up and put my hands on his chest. When my fingers brush against his smooth, chiseled skin, he pushes them away. "Behave, Ms. Kent. If you need something, you have to ask and ask nicely."

I can't take my eyes away from his perfect chest as I ask, "Dr. Carroway?" I flush at the heavy rasp present in my voice that gives immediate notice of how turned on I am by this little game.

"Yes?"

"I'm hurting," I whimper pathetically

"Oh? And where are you hurting, Ms. Kent?" This game is giving him authority over me—a slight domination that I'm finding incredibly arousing from my usually sweet lover, and my skin tingles with the heady knowledge that even more good things await me. "I may be able to alleviate any discomfort you're feeling." Picking up his hand, I set it on my chest, satisfaction filling me as I watch his eyes darken with lust. His jaw flexes when my eyes make contact with his tented pants, the taut seam of his trousers restricting it.

"Here," I tell him, and watch him lick his lips while staring at mine. I love him so much in this moment. I've had so much difficulty with our current reality that we needed to step outside the bounds of reality and have some fun. His comfort allows me to explore my sexuality safely and build my confidence.

"I'll take this into consideration. Tell me though, what is your biggest ailment? Is it this?" he asks, flicking my bra open suddenly with the front clasp that I'm thanking my lucky stars that this bra possesses. He runs a finger lightly over my nipple before pinching it suddenly and sending shivers all over my body.

With his other hand, he pushes his pants down. I immediately take advantage of the situation and push his underwear aside, taking him in my hand and squeezing.

"Is anything else bothering you?" he asks, his voice deeper than normal as I work him over. The rush of his breath fans my cheek as he dips down to my ear. "Does it make you wet when I boss you around, pretty girl?" He nips my lobe until my pulse is pounding in my throat. "I've wanted you on the tip of my tongue for weeks, and it's time I get my fill."

I whimper and the façade falls for just a second as I sink into his chest.

"Let me taste you," he whispers.

Moving my hand off of him, he guides my fingers behind my thong. "Are you wet?" I groan as I feel my way along the silk glide of my skin. Warm and lush, I slide farther down and coat my fingers in the evidence of my arousal.

"Yes." Without thought, I bring the proof to his mouth, and he sucks my fingers with a deep moan. Teasing with his tongue, he flicks the tips as he would my clit, and my legs grow weak at the thought of him taking and tasting me.

He closes his eyes, counts to three and drops my hand. "In bed, Ms. Kent, now." I'm happy to submit to his will...but I suddenly get the urge to have a little of my own. Before he can comply, I strip him of his doctor's jacket and his briefs, and then guide him to my California King spread out before us. With the slightest touch, I push him to the mattress and he free falls, knees over the edge. Breaking from character for just a minute, he unleashes the concerned side of him. "If you are in pain or re-injure yourself for even one second, we're not having sex for a year. Got it, Ari?"

"Are you done, Dr. Carroway?"

"Yes," he says, giving me a seductive smirk at my impertinence.

"Good, because I'm ready for you." He growls and sits, hauling me into his chest.

"That's what I like to hear," he says triumphantly. He falls back to the bed with me in his arms, and I squeal. "Get up here, pretty girl. I want you to reward me for my house call."

I pop up on my elbow. "You do deserve some thanks for your services." I kiss him until we're both panting and my hand is wrapped around his pulsing erection.

"Ugh," he grunts when I pull up and then run my palm up to the tip.

"You know...I think that I decided on how you can reward me. Up," he orders me. He tugs on my hip, and I kneel next to him. "Swing your leg over my shoulder."

"No." My brow falls, and I shake my head. "Absolutely no way."

He growls and drags me up and over with such force that I fall forward, my hair splayed around my hands as they grip the sheets. "Jesse," I whisper, breathless from the fall and his nose that brushes along my dampened panties. Biting the meat of my inner thigh, he sinks his teeth into my flesh and marks me as his.

I hiss when his tongue makes its first drag. He's wrenched

away the silk and is taking his time to lick the length of me. Once, twice, and he groans, pulling me down onto his face. Gripping the tiny lace thong, he rips it off and owns my hips, wrapping his arm around one to manage my movement. And I move, swaying into the rhythm of his mouth, as he gets hungrier with each pass. I realize this position allows me my own modicum of control. He's letting me set the pace, and I do. Sitting up, I fist his hair and tip my head back when the vibration of his growl reaches my clit, and a feverish pulse takes over all thought. My skin lights up, vibrating—every nerve is aware of each flick of his tongue and every sweep of his lips.

I love your mouth, your marvelous, skilled fucking mouth. I love it on me. When he laughs, I realize I said it out loud and I don't care—it's the truth. The vibration becomes delicate, and the air pricks at each nerve, lighting my skin and opening me to pleasure. My hips rotate on him and with him as he flicks and pushes me higher, so high that I'm not sure I'll survive the climb, let alone the fall. It feels so damn good.

Too good, it's too much, too fast.

Just when I'm afraid of it, afraid of the intensity, and cry out, "Stop, no, please" he takes me in. Sucking, he holds me to him so I have nowhere to go but to fall forward and down, down, down. I scream into the mattress and jerk against him as I crash over and over again. His murmured appreciation chases my orgasm and reheats it, lapping against my sensitivity until I'm tensed for another one. He follows me with a groan when my body naturally wrenches away from the white-hot bliss, yet my hand is fisted so tight in his hair, I drag him with me at the same time. It's a duel with only one possible ending and he beats it from me with the flattened edge of his wicked tongue.

Slow, bleating whimpers are pushed into the bed as he shows no mercy and demands every ounce of my pleasure. "Jesse," I whisper more than once as I find myself somewhere amongst the ruin and crawl back down to lie on top of him. I press kisses along his forehead, cheek and jaw, murmuring "So good" and "I love your mouth" until mine takes his. I find myself there, my sweet musk mixing with his, and I drown in it. Snaking my hand between our bodies, I find him. Silk and steel melt into my hand as I stroke up and down, swallowing his groans as I want to swallow him. He breaks away, pushing until I'm flat on my back.

"I want you," he grounds out between his teeth. The passion of the moment is raging behind his intense gaze. I don't dare deny him and slide further up on the bed, spreading my legs as I go. He's on his knees in a heartbeat, savage and stalking forward, pinning me down with his eyes. I'd give him anything and everything, and he knows it. He plans on taking it.

"Please."

"Please what?" He runs his hand along my thigh and bends to deepen the outline of the mark he made earlier with his teeth. Looking at me through his lashes he says, "Please touch you, or please make you come again?"

"Both."

He grins and straightens, finding the perfect position between my thighs. His wild, undone smirk falls away when he throws his head back and lunges inside of me in one, deep thrust. I lose my breath when he fills me up and stills for the shortest moment, the moment when I feel replete and want for nothing, until the second it all changes and I need him to move. I need to fear his withdrawal only to feel the fullness once more. He holds me open with his hand digging into my leg, and I wrap the other around his ass and hold on for dear life. Holy hell, I've forgotten what it's like when he's wild and loses himself so thoroughly inside of me. It feels so, so good— he feels good. His body takes over, pounding into a punishing tempo. He's punishing me for what's happened to us and for making him wait so long to feel this free and good and mine.

Bending down, he braces his elbow next to my ear so he can find my mouth and destroy that too. My breath comes in panting waves, a mirror of his, and our eyes lock. I watch his lips part and his head tip back as he slides in and out in long, deep strokes. My hips meet his as we come together until I need more. Faster and deeper, and then my nails rake down his back, and he bucks into me with a hiss and stills.

"No," I cry out, on the edge of something far too good to lose.

"Do you have something to ask your doctor?" he asks with the utmost constraint, a sassy-ass smirk lifting the corner of his mouth. My heart pounds in time with the now missing beat of his hips.

"Don't stop." I dig my fingers into his backside.

"No?" His lids fall to half-mast, and his voice goes with it, sexy as hell. No longer just commanding, but playful, and my skin tingles, as if he's touched me everywhere. "My naughty patient, do you want your examination to conclude?"

"Please, don't play with me."

I can't say any more, but if I could I'd tell him how good he feels in me, around me, rubbing all over me. My nipples spike into taut beads as they rise up and into his chest. "Please."

He smiles, a full-blown I-will-rock-your-world-and-you'll-beg-for-more grin. "Don't play with you? Isn't that what had you so hot earlier? Playing?" Pushing in deeper, he dips to my ear and whispers, "Do you want me to keep going?" As if testing my resolve, he leans on his side, his face remaining hot as hell, and reaches with his other hand to lift my leg around his hip so I'm cradling him in a vice grip. Holding very still, he says, "I'm waiting."

I'm so distracted. "Huh? What?" I say, breathless, and not at all ashamed to admit how bad I need him to move.

"How was your visit today? Your doctor's satisfaction scores depend on your answer." I try to smile and play along, but it disappears when he bites my neck. My body starts pulsing around him, uncaring he's chosen not to move. He groans, all sass wiped away, and he rocks into me. Slow and sweet, the friction rubs in the most delicious way. I wrap myself around him, licking and sucking his neck and the dip above his collarbone as my fingers explore. I revel in the taut lines of his back and ass that flex as his strokes become more powerful. He is mine. Always and forever mine. With that thought, the pulse turns into a tremor, and the rhythm of an orgasm taps an ambient chill up my spine. It unfurls into a blinding light behind my eyes, and I give in, letting it roll through me and around him.

"Jesse, I love you," I groan, at first clamoring to crawl closer and then arching away when the waves of sensation threaten to break me in two. He feeds on my breasts, taking my nipple into his mouth and then clamping down as his breath punches around it. He cries out and slides into the hollow of my neck, where I take in the scream of his release as his thrusts become long and sharp a moment before he relaxes against me. I kiss him everywhere, tasting the two of us on his skin, his face, and neck.

And then for some reason, the images hit me. Over and over they come at me, until I'm overwhelmed and not sure that I can escape them.

Closing my eyes, I block it all out: The hotel room with Gentry's present, my injury, the whirlwind of the last few months, Gentry and that fucking gun. I roll to my back and hide under my arms, caging myself beneath them.

"Hey, what's going on in there?" It's a soft question, but I'm feeling hard, and for whatever reason, I'm ready to fight. To prevent that from happening, I remain silent. "Talk to me, Ari."

"Nothing is going on. I'm fine."

"You don't sound fine."

"I am. I'm just tired, and I want to go to bed."

A long pause—no sound, no movement, no nothing. I'm shutting him out again, just as I have been for months. I know it, and he does too. It doesn't feel good, and my skin prickles with unease and the itch to make it better. I'm mad, and I'm not sure why. That's not true. If I think about it, the simple question has a great big answer—I'm fucking raging-at-the-world mad about everything. Take your pick: Being trapped in this house, Jensen and Tanner's avoidance of me, Gentry and his gun, and that stupid fucking hotel room for bringing the past so close to the present. I'm a stranger in my own life.

Everything is eating away at me, every day, every minute—the hole in my heart grows wider, and I see Gentry every time I close my eyes.

Fear. Fear has woven into my heart and is slowly suffocating me. I can't eat. I can't sleep because when I try, Gentry's eyes are staring at me and I'm afraid next time it will be the guys that get those bullets.

6
THEN

ARIANA

None of the guys are in school today. I check my phone for the millionth time, but there's no messages waiting for me. I haven't texted them, always afraid that they won't want to hear from me after a lifetime of the people in my life constantly feeling that way.

Finally, when none of them are there at the end of school, I can't help but type out a quick text to Jesse.

Everything okay? Missing you.

I send it before I can change my mind. Jesse's response is almost immediate.

Dealing with something.

There's a pause as I think about what to say, and suddenly, he's calling me. "Hey," I say eagerly.

"I hate to ask you to do this, but we need your help with Tanner," he says quietly.

"What can I do?" I answer quickly.

"Are you still at the school?"

"Yes."

"Be there in five," he responds before hanging up. My mind is racing about what could be wrong. What did they need my help with? What had Tanner done that they were dealing with? Was it drugs again?

Jesse pulls up in his truck about fifteen minutes later. He quickly gets out of the car and opens the door for me.

I can see the stress written across his face.

"Tanner isn't in a good place. And he's not letting Jensen and I help him. We're hoping that he'll listen to you," Jesse says as we begin to drive, shooting a quick look at me to see my reaction.

"What do you mean that he's not in a good place?" I ask.

"It's something that Tanner will have to tell you when he's ready. But let's just say that his family makes Jensen's family look like the '*Leave it to Beaver*' family compared to them."

I feel a little ashamed in this moment. They've started opening up to me, but I haven't given them any details about what my life at home is like. For some reason, it's just really hard to share things like that. It's a shame that I carry with me everywhere, and I don't want this one good thing I've found to be tainted by it.

"Do you think that we ever really recover from the damage that our families do to us?" I ask him, staring at the trees as we pass them by. Jesse is racing, so they're just a blur. We pull up to the outside of the bar, a bar that I had ironically been in before to come collect my mother. If Tanner was in there, he definitely wasn't in a good place. I had no doubt in my mind that this place had no problem handing out alcohol to minors.

"I'm really sorry about this," Jesse says as we sit there for a moment, looking at the dilapidated state of the bar. He reaches over and grabs my hand and squeezes it, bringing it to his lips to brush a kiss across it. Despite the situation, I can't help but get tingles at his touch. I soak up any physical contact I can get from them, like I'm a plant that desperately needs water in the sun. Jesse gets caught up in my eyes as he's kissing my hand, and it's the strangest sensation to have someone looking at me so intently.

He shakes his head suddenly, like he's snapping himself out of whatever trance he had just been in. "Ready?" he asks, opening his door.

I take a deep breath and nod. I was well versed in saving drunk people, unfortunately. It was the underlying cause of the drunkenness that I hadn't figured out a way to fix thus far.

As soon as the door to the bar opened, I was hit by a wave of sweaty, smelly heat. Greasy food mixed with the stench of beer wasn't the best smell. Combine that with the stench of body odor, and it could make you vomit. As we walk across the faded wood plank floor, my shoes keep getting stuck on sticky portions of the floor where alcohol had been spilled and never cleaned up.

It was impossible to miss Tanner. He's three sheets to the wind and has somehow ended up with a bottle of whiskey. He's swaying on the far side of the room, dancing to the taciturn beats of whatever old rock song is playing. Jensen is propped on a chair at a table nearby, looking annoyed as a couple of barflies try to talk to him. Tanner is surrounded by a few haggard looking cougars that have definitely seen better days, but he doesn't seem to know that they exist. He's so caught up in his own little world.

"Um, how do you want to do this? What exactly am I supposed to be doing?" I whisper to Jesse.

"I'll take care of the ladies," he grimaces. "You just see if you can get Tanner to leave with you. Wait here a second while I distract them," he adds.

I watch as Jesse transforms into his stage persona, putting on a sexy smirk and what I would call bedroom eyes as he approaches the two cougars, who look like they are about to devour Tanner whole. Jensen looks up hopefully when he sees Jesse, and then his attention flashes to me. He doesn't look happy that I'm here, and I wonder what that's about. Had Jesse come to get me without consulting Jensen? Was this going to create issues that I was here?

Deciding to stop doubting myself, I begin to walk towards the still dancing Tanner. Jesse has successfully caught the ladies' attentions, and now they are trying to paw at him. Tanner would owe him after this.

I get to Tanner and stand there for a second, waiting for him to notice me. It takes a second before the chorus of the current song has him doing some kind of complicated spin move that puts me in his line of sight.

"Princess," he slurs, surprising me when he grabs me right away and pulls me into a hug that is more of the dance, since he hasn't stopped moving. "I didn't snort anything," he says proudly, his eyes flickering over me affectionately.

"Good boy," I say as I awkwardly pat him. I guess that is an improvement, if he hasn't immediately turned to white powder in order to help him forget.

"I'm so glad you're here," he tells me as he pulls me against his chest. I dance with him for a couple more minutes, only wincing slightly when he steps on my feet as he weaves us around drunkenly. He's acting carefree, but I can see the tiredness around his eyes. There's a desperation in his actions, he just wants to forget. And I don't blame him for that. If I wasn't constantly surrounded by two people who have made my life hell because of excess drinking and drugs, I would be right there with him.

"We should get out of here," I tell him when the song we had been dancing to finally ends.

My eyes widen as the hand on my back starts to trail down until he's squeezing my ass. I quickly yank his hand back up, not wanting him to have regrets whenever he sobers up. Not that I mind his hand on my ass. I just want him to actually be aware that he's doing it to me when it happens.

I mean, if it happens.

I step away from him, holding on to one of his hands.

"Don't you want to keep dancing?" he asks adorably, trying to show off some other kind of dance move that I recognize as one that he uses on stage. Somehow, even as drunken off balance as he is, he still manages to look sexy doing it.

"I kind of want to get some food," I tell him, trying to think up excuses to leave.

"My girl's hungry?" he asks, suddenly flinging the hand I wasn't holding into the air. "Yo, Ron. Can you get my lady some nachos?" he yells out to a grizzled looking barkeeper that doesn't look like he has bathed in quite some time. I definitely didn't want him preparing any food that I ate.

"That's okay," I call out, looking around to see if Jesse or Jensen can help me. Jesse looks alarmed as the two women he has been entertaining look to be getting more and more aggressive. I grimace when I see one of them reach out and try to grab his crotch. Looking to Jensen next, I see that he is just sitting there watching Tanner and I, continuing to ignore the women who are trying to talk to him.

I wave at him, trying to give my best "help me out here" look. He shoots me a thumbs up and then turns his attention to his phone, apparently leaving me on my own to deal with Tanner. What was his problem?

"Tanner, I need your help with something. Can you come with me outside?" I finally try. Astonishing me, he immediately snaps to attention and starts to stride towards the door, dragging me along. I shoot a look back at Jesse and Jensen to make sure they see that we are leaving. They're both watching us leave, looking a mixture of relieved and flabbergasted.

As soon as we are outside, Tanner stops walking and turns to look at me. "What do you need, Princess?" he slurs. "Who do I need to beat up?"

The funny thing is that he actually looks like he means it. He's prepared to march off to be my knight in shining armor, even as he tries to beat his own demons.

"Let's go somewhere else to talk. I don't have good memories of this place," I tell him honestly, thinking about the last time that I pried my mother from this place. She'd been trying to service someone in the middle of the bar, and as bad as this place was, evidently, they didn't want the police called since she was also asking for payment for the services she was trying to perform.

"Why are you staring at me like this?" I whisper, noticing him watching me intently. My voice sounds funny as the words leave my lips.

"Princess, I always thought that I didn't deserve anything good to happen to me. I've been told for so long that I'm nothing, that I'm unwanted, that I'm trash that my dad wished he could get rid of, that I've believed it for longer than I can remember."

Those silver eyes stay locked on mine, even as his trembling hand reaches out towards my face.

"And now…now what do you believe?" I ask, my voice barely a whisper as I soak up his touch as he gently strokes my cheek.

"And now I'm starting to doubt that I'm really that worthless, Princess. Because good things like you wouldn't happen to someone worthless. You're my good thing, Princess. As long as I have you, that can't possibly be true."

I watch as a tear slides down his face. I somehow know that Tanner Crosby is not someone that cries easily, that the solitary tear he just wept is something that should be treasured, something that should be remembered.

He's my good thing too. They all are.

"I'm really tired, Princess," he says, his voice slurring once again as his brief moment of lucidity disappears.

"Me too," I whisper back to him, thinking of how worn down life can make you.

Jesse and Jensen choose that moment to make an appearance.

"Let's get out of here," says Jensen gruffly.

"We can go to my house. My parents are out of town so they won't notice this mess," says Jesse, gesturing to Tanner. I nod, relieved that we have somewhere to go.

For a long time, I didn't have anywhere to go or anyone to go with. I'm glad that Tanner has had them, and that I have them now too.

I'd go with them anywhere.

7
NOW

ARIANA

I'm caught between a burning desire to get out of the house, and a fear that I'll have another panic attack and freak out again like I have been. Finally, I decide I need to see a therapist.

"You're getting better every day," says Jensen when I broach the subject with him. I feel like we need to get someone that the band's team trusts, just because I wouldn't put it past someone to try and make a quick buck on what I'm dealing with, so I've asked the guys to get some recommendations for therapists. I can already see the headline now about "The Sound of Us's crazy girlfriend losing it." Evidently, the guys are not happy about me wanting to talk to someone.

"I'm not getting better at all," I tell him. "My body might be healing, but my head isn't."

"Baby, it's all going to be fine."

"I'm not fine." I slam my empty glass on the counter in front of me. "I haven't slept in weeks, I can barely eat. I fluctuate between wanting to stay locked in this house and wanting to run away. A fireworks display has me cowering. Not to mention that you and Tanner are hardly speaking to me, and Jesse is constantly sending me worried looks. I am not okay. We are not okay."

There's a pause after that. "I haven't been avoiding you," he says finally. I throw my hands in the air, well aware that I'm being unreasonable but not able to control myself.

"Okay, maybe I have, but it hasn't felt like that. I'm always thinking about you, wanting to be with you, watching you even when you aren't paying attention. I'm just fucking messed up about what happened, Ari," he says in a voice that sounds broken. "I watched him shoot you, and there was nothing I could do to save you. I sat in that hospital room and held your hand, and there was nothing I could do to wake you up. I'm scared to go back to our regular lives because I know now that I can't protect you, I can't save you when it comes down to it. And I don't know how to handle that feeling."

I've been so wrapped up in my own pain that I haven't seen how much they are still suffering. I knew that they weren't doing well in the hospital, but I guess I thought that they had gotten better since being here. Obviously, I was wrong.

"Is that what's bothering Tanner too?" I ask quietly. Jensen just sighs and takes a pull of his beer. "Tanner has his own issues because of the fact that Gentry was getting information from Miranda because she was jealous of you and wanted Tanner. He's all sorts of fucked up because of how guilty he feels."

They told me about Miranda in the hospital. I couldn't believe that their own manager put us all in so much danger, just because she was interested in Tanner. I opened my mouth to say something and Jensen shakes his head. "He should have told us how much she was coming on to him, but I've told him a million times that it isn't his fault. Gentry would have found a way to come after you, no matter what."

I nod, agreeing with that.

"Baby, I can't sleep either," Jensen says, setting his beer down and pulling me into his embrace. "I lie awake at night, just thinking about the fact that Gentry is still out there, that they haven't found him yet."

I feel him shiver against me. "The label wants us back on tour asap. They're setting up a concert in LA in two weeks. And I don't know how I'm going to do that show. I don't want you in public, yet I can't bear to be away from you."

This is the first I'm hearing about them having a show or returning back to the tour, but I'm not surprised by the news. I knew that the label was going to be pushing for the tour to resume as soon as possible. I'm surprised the guys were able to get away for this long.

"Maybe we should all go see a therapist," I suggest softly, but Jensen is already shaking his head.

"The only thing I need is your safety. That's the only thing that's going to get me better," he says stubbornly, and I sigh, burrowing my head into his chest, inhaling his scent that will always be home to me.

I end up finding a therapist without the guys, thanks to Clark helping me out with a name. He's been operating as the band's de facto manager along with being their agent as they look for a manager to replace Miranda. Lately, he's been stopping by more and more for meetings with the guys as they get ready to start touring again, but he always stops to talk to me when they're done. I used to think he was a bit creepy, but I've come to realize that he's just awkward but well meaning. When he asked me this last time how I was doing, I just went for it, deciding to ask him for suggestions. That morning, I started crying after Tanner dropped a glass bottle and the sound of the glass hitting the floor scared me. I couldn't keep living like this.

Clark actually had a bunch of names to give me, as his clients frequently needed therapy after the rigors of touring. I decided I would feel more comfortable talking to a female therapist and called and set up an appointment that day.

So here I am now, waiting in a luxurious lobby to talk to Dr. Mayfield for my first appointment.

"Ariana," calls a pleasant voice as a sharply dressed blonde steps through a door on the far side of the room. She's a striking woman, probably in her mid-40s with brilliant green eyes. I'm dressed in black tights and an oversized sweater, my hair in a ponytail, and my face is devoid of any makeup. I immediately feel like I should have dressed nicer for the appointment. The warm smile she gives me helps settle my nerves, however.

She shakes my hand and introduces herself, and I follow her into her office. The office is much tidier than I thought it would be. For some reason when I imagined going to therapy, I imagined it taking place in a crowded room with lots of old books and a long leather couch. Instead, there's hardly anything in the room. A rug and two comfy looking armchairs are set up in the middle of the room, and there's a few potted plants in three of the corners. Other than that, the room's bare.

We settle in, and I shift in my seat nervously under her patient gaze. She observes me for what seems like a full minute before speaking. "What can I help you with?" she finally asks gently.

It's hard to open up now that I'm here. I know that she's signed an NDA, and that she comes highly recommended by the label, but she's still a stranger. But maybe that's what I need, an outside opinion.

After giving myself a little pep talk, I begin. The words fall fast and furious from me. I talk about high school and meeting the guys, I talk about Gentry, and reuniting with the guys. I talk about going on tour and Gentry stalking us-to her credit she doesn't even blink with the news that I am in a relationship with all three of them. I talk about everything but the reason that I didn't follow the guys to LA I don't know that I'll ever be able to do that. Thankfully, she doesn't ask anything about that. Instead, she focuses on what's been going on lately, how I'm feeling, and the panic attacks I've been suffering from.

"Ariana," she finally says, after she's listened to me more. "You've talked a lot about things that you've done with your men. You've talked about the tour, and supporting them. You've talked about how much you're worried about how they're handling everything. What I want to know is what you're doing for yourself. I want to know what you want."

I open my mouth to answer, but no words come out.

"I thought so," she responds. "Ariana, have you ever actually done something for yourself in your entire life?"

"Leaving Gentry was for me," I finally am able to respond. But she just shakes her head.

"Would you have had the strength to leave if you hadn't won those tickets and the guys hadn't pushed for you to stay with them?"

Again, I don't have a quick answer. "I would like to think that I would have. But it wasn't like it was easy to get away," I answer somewhat defensively, not wanting to envision a life where I had never been able to leave Gentry until he finally went too far and killed me.

"Ariana..." she begins gently. For some reason, I begin holding my breath, knowing that whatever she is going to say next is going to hurt. "I think you're stuck. From the time you were a teenager, you've always been living for someone else. I don't think you really know who you are, what you want out of life. And until you figure that out, until you start living for you and not someone else... You're always going to have issues. What you're experiencing right now isn't just panic attacks because of your fear that your ex-husband is going to attack you again. What you are experiencing is a feeling that you've lost control of your life. So the question is, what are you going to do about that?"

I sit there silently, weighing her words. My first instinct is to deny that she's right, to tell her she doesn't really know anything about me and couldn't possibly understand what I've been through and why I am the way that I am. I know what I want, don't I? I mean, I at least know I want Jesse, Tanner, and Jensen and I want them forever. But what did that mean if that was the only thing that I knew I want in my life? I want freedom... but what did freedom mean? I want to stand on my own two feet, but what does that look like? I want to contribute more to my relationship, but how do I do that? The more I think about it, sitting in this chair under the doctor's watchful gaze, the more I know she's right. I have no idea who Ariana Kent is. And until I figure that out, I'm never going to be happy.

8
NOW

ARIANA

I'm still playing the doctor's words in my head when I get back to Jesse's mansion. Jesse wanted to go with me to the appointment, but I'd forced him to stay home, knowing that I needed to do at least this first appointment on my own. The fact that I considered letting Jesse go with me though, seems to play right into the doctor's thoughts about me.

Jensen's waiting in the front entryway as I walk through the door. He looks exhausted, which probably isn't a good thing considering that the guys have their concert tonight. I thought having a therapy session today would probably be best, as the concert is probably going to bring up some bad memories considering the last concert I attended I almost died. Jensen looks relieved to see me, almost as if he was afraid that I wouldn't come back. He rushes towards me, and pulls me into his arms. He's dressed in nothing but a pair of sweatpants that dips dangerously low, and the combination of his perfect abs and that delicious V that all three of them possess has my mind short-circuiting.

"I feel like this is all our fault," he says, kissing me sadly.

"What's your fault?" I ask, feeling confused.

"Because we've broken you, and we swore we never would. You're having to go to a therapist because we can't figure out how to fix this. You're my life, Ariana. More important than anything. Yet here I am, dragging you to this shitty concert tonight because I'm a selfish asshole who can't bear to be away from you." His forehead falls to mine. "Tell me what I can do so you won't wake up screaming on the few occasions you do sleep? How can I ease your stomach so you can eat? Tell me how to fix us, so you don't have to run to a therapist to try and fix your life."

"Jensen, going to a therapist isn't a bad thing. Why are you so hung up on the fact that I went?" I ask, growing annoyed at the pity party he's got going on.

He opens his mouth to answer, but just then, a voice from my past all of a sudden comes barreling down the hall.

I push back from Jensen, startled by that voice, the voice of easing anxiety, late-night chats, and hysterical giggles. "That sounds like..." I whisper as footsteps and the voice grow louder in the hall, nearing the front entryway where we are still standing. "Amberlie."

I look at Jensen in disbelief. He looks torn between wanting to finish our conversation and wanting to let me reunite with Amberlie.

"I haven't talked to her in years," I whisper, excitement and trepidation coursing through my veins as I wait for her to come into view.

A second later, she's hustling down the hallway, still the ball of energy that I remembered her to be.

"Ari," she screeches before she's running into me, practically knocking me down with her enthusiasm. I'm crying, not believing that she's really here. To be quite honest, I was a terrible friend in the end. After everything happened, and I decided not to go to LA, I cut everything off...everything, including my best friend. She tried and tried to talk to me, to be there for me, but I rejected every effort she made. Eventually, her calls stopped. The last I heard she had gotten married to Teddy, a guy she started dating senior year who went to State College with her, and now she was living two towns over with him.

Looking at her, she was the same Amberlie. A little curvier than she had been, but it only enhanced that glow that she always seemed to possess. Her hair was a shade darker than it had been, and her makeup was more natural than it had been in high school. She's a knockout.

I realized after I had been staring an awkwardly long amount of time at her that she was studying me with the same intensity that I was studying her.

Suddenly, she whirled around and glared at the guys. Jesse and Tanner followed Amberlie down the hall and were watching our reunion with Jensen now.

"What's wrong with her?" she hisses at them. Their faces all turn guilty, even though they haven't actually done anything wrong.

"I can't believe you're here," I tell her, diverting her attention. She turns back to me, her face lighting up as we once again hug each other tightly.

"I've been trying to get in contact with the guys since the news erupted with the story that you had been shot. It took a while to get past the suits and get any news about how you were doing." Her eyes turn glassy with tears. "I can't believe you were shot. I can't believe you were shot by your husband. I didn't even know you were married. You didn't even invite me to the wedding." Amberlie's voice is nearly hysterical by the end as she rambles on, and I'm feeling guiltier than ever about how I treated my best friend five years ago. Amberlie was the first friend that I actually ever had, and she deserved better from me.

"It's a long story," I tell her softly. "And I know that 'sorry' falls extremely short for everything I owe you, but I am so glad you're here."

Amberlie melts and throws her arms around me. I'm suddenly aware that the guys are still standing there, witnesses to our moment.

"I know you two have a lot to catch up with, but we need to leave for the concert in thirty minutes," Jensen says gruffly. And I nod at him, having a tough time speaking at the moment since I'm so choked up with emotion.

"Let's go upstairs so I can change," I finally squeak out to Amberlie, who immediately links arms with me so that we ascend the stairs side by side. "We'll be right down," I tell the guys, who are still watching us. Tanner looks almost a bit jealous right now that Amberlie's here, which is stupid since he's been the one choosing not to spend time with me, when I've been right at his fingertips for months.

We get to my room, and Amberlie squeals as she examines everything. "I always knew this was going to be your life," she tells me excitedly. "I knew that there wasn't a future that didn't end with you and the guys together." She visibly swoons when she sits down on my bed and feels how comfortable it is.

"I've got to have Teddy get us one of these mattresses," she says. "It's amazing."

"How is Teddy?" I ask and her face visibly brightens, even though I wasn't sure that was possible.

"He's still Teddy," she sighs dreamily. "I still wake up every day thanking the heavens that he's mine. And Cody looks just like him," she tells me, digging into her purse for something.

"Cody?" I ask, and I watch as a flash of sadness crosses her features.

"Cody's my son. I had almost forgotten that you haven't met him, since it feels like he's been mine forever. He's three years old and just a handful, but we wouldn't have it any other way," she tells me, and I know that she looks sad because I should have known that. I should have been there, visiting her in the hospital when the baby was born. I should have been at his birthday parties, his christening...I should have been there.

She holds out the picture, and I examine the cutest little kid that I've ever seen. He's got the same auburn hair as Amberlie did in high school with bright blue eyes. He's perfect.

"I can't wait for you to meet him," she tells me, and I nod, feeling emotional again at all the life that I've lost.

I take a shuddery breath and give her a watery smile. "I can't wait to meet him. He's the most perfect little boy that I've ever seen."

"Isn't he?" she squeals, taking the picture back from me and smiling at it fondly. Before we can say anything else, the room is filled with Jesse's voice as he talks through the speaker that's in every room. The house is so big that it would be impossible to talk to someone on the other side of the house without the speaker system.

"Ladies, we need to get going," he says, and I quickly run into my closet to get some clothes. "Coming," I respond, as I look for something to wear. It's a fine line being the girlfriend of the biggest band in the world. I have to look edgy and sexy without looking slutty. It's actually not an easy feat.

Amberlie walks into the closet, looking a little awestruck at the sight. The closet is about the size of the trailer I grew up in, and the guys have stuffed it full of more clothes than I'm pretty sure that I could wear in three lifetimes. She begins to look around as I start pulling tops from hangers that could potentially work.

"What about this?" she says, and I turn around to see that she's holding up my leather skirt, the one that I wore that first concert. It feels like a lifetime ago, even though it hasn't been that long. That skirt reminds me of times when I've been brave, when my life has changed dramatically. It feels perfect for tonight.

A few minutes later, I'm dressed in the skirt that I'm wearing over a black, lacey, long-sleeve bodysuit.

"You look perfect," she says admiringly, smoothing down a section of my hair. "And so skinny," she continues, a little bit self-consciously.

"I think motherhood has only made you more beautiful," I tell her meaningfully, and she must believe me, because she immediately brightens. "Let's get down to your boys. I'm sure they are freaking out about how long we're taking," she says, sounding happy again.

We go downstairs, and sure enough, all the guys are waiting at the foot of the stairs impatiently. I lose my train of thought again at the sight of them all together, dressed for the concert. On the tour, they usually get ready in their dressing rooms but I guess they decided to just get ready here tonight.

Jesse is wearing a velvet blazer with nothing on underneath and a pair of tight fitting black jeans. My mouth waters looking at him. It somehow feels even more decadent knowing that his nipple piercings are waiting just out of sight. Jensen and Tanner look equally delicious. Jensen is wearing a tight black shirt that accentuates every line on his chest and abs with a pair of grey skinny jeans, and Tanner is wearing a loose white tank shirt with leather pants, his tattoos mouthwatering. The effect of all three of them is effectively mind-blowing, and I wonder how it is that they continue to get more attractive to me.

"I think I've somehow died and gone to hot guy heaven," says Amberlie. "Either that, or I'm dreaming. Pinch me, so I can wake up before Teddy gets mad at me for drooling in my sleep."

Her comments break the spell I was under, and we all laugh before heading outside to where the guys' customary black SUV is waiting for us. Tanner surprises me by putting his arm around my waist and pulling me into his side. "You are so fucking hot," he tells me, licking the side of my neck. My whole body feels like I've caught fire. I probably should be mad at him that he's been basically hiding from me lately and now he's all over me, but Tanner and his silver eyes have always been a weakness of mine. There's not much I wouldn't do for him, wouldn't do for all three of them.

Amberlie and the guys manage to keep me distracted on the way to the venue, but when the outside of the Hollywood Bowl comes into view, I start to feel like I might faint.

BOOM. Gentry's standing there with the gun. BOOM. Pain is slicing across my body.

"Ari," Jensen's voice slices through the darkness. My eyes fly open, and I find myself sprawled against the leather seats. The SUV is sitting in the parking lot by the artist entrance, and the guys and Amberlie are all hovered around me looking concerned. I fainted.

Shit.

"That's it, we're going home," barks Tanner with a curse. And that's enough to bring me fully back to life. I sit up quickly, ignoring the headrush that I get when I do so.

"No. I'm fine. I have to do this," I tell them firmly, or as firmly as one can when they've just regained consciousness. We talked at my appointment about the triggers that I might encounter tonight, and Dr. Mayfield stressed that I should try and push through them, or it might build up my fear even more in my mind. I have to do this.

The guys are arguing, but I don't wait for them to make a decision for me. Instead, I grab Amberlie and head towards the door that leads inside, my security team-who had been following us in another SUV-hustling to catch up with me. Right as I reach for the door I get the strangest feeling that I'm being watched. I turn around and scan the parking lot, but as far as I can see, there's no one around.

I'm just being paranoid, I tell myself. "Keep your eyes out tonight," I needlessly remind my team, and they all nod, making me feel slightly better.

By this time, the guys have hustled to catch up with us. Tanner's scowling at me, Jesse looks worried, and Jensen looks like he's about to punch someone...most likely Tanner.

"You've got to let me do this," I tell them, and after what seems like an hour but is most likely just a few seconds, they each reluctantly nod.

After that, there's no time to discuss anything because the guys are being swept down the hall for soundcheck since we're running late. Amberlie and I, along with my security team, are led by a venue employee back to the green room. As I settle down on the couch with Amberlie and we start discussing some of the shows that I've seen on the tour, I can't help but think at how different the room looks from that first one back in South Carolina. There aren't any strung out groupies hanging out, it doesn't feel like a party's about to break out. It feels chill, comfortable...like what I would want a green room to feel like if this was my concert.

I wonder if the guys hate it.

Pushing the self-doubt out of my mind, I try and focus on the story that Amberlie is telling. It's time I stop living in my head so much and concentrate on the present. It's time I actually start living.

9
THEN

ARIANA

Tanner hasn't come to school this week. He hasn't come to band practice, he hasn't answered our calls. I want to go over there, but the guys won't let me. Jensen and Jesse drove over to Tanner's house, but Tanner wouldn't let them through the gates, only telling them that he needed a break and he'd see them next week.

My stomach hurt all week thinking about him all alone in that gigantic house. I still had no idea what was going on behind the scenes with his family, but I wasn't an idiot. I knew it was bad. My stomach continued to hurt all week as I anticipated the worst.

It wasn't until 11 PM, two days later, that I finally heard from Tanner.

"I need you," the text read. And even though I had already changed into sleep shorts and a tank top, I quickly pulled on some jeans. "I'm here. Whatever you need," I write back.

"I'll pick you up at our usual spot," he responds, since the guys had gotten used to picking me up on the county road outside the trailer park instead of where I lived.

He's already sitting there when I walk out to the road, and my eyes widen in surprise. Evidently, he was waiting for me. He doesn't get out of the car like usual to open the door, so I hop in, worry churning in my gut. I take a deep inhale in shock. He looks awful. Like he's been on a bender and got into a fight. His beautiful face is mottled with black and blue bruises, and his eyes are bloodshot. There's a cut on his forehead that's been stitched up.

"Oh, Tanner," I say, tears woven throughout my voice.

"Don't worry about me, Princess. I'm alright. I've just missed you," he tells me.

"I've missed you too," I tell him, grabbing his hand and holding it to my heart. I kiss his knuckles, noticing that they're bruised and cracked as well.

"Want to go somewhere with me?" he asks. And I nod, because I would follow him anywhere. Tanner should know by now that my answer is always yes when it comes to him...when it comes to them in general. We drive to the next town over and stop at a tattoo shop that I've passed before on our way to the lake. It's now midnight, but it looks to be still open.

"You're getting a tattoo?" I ask.

He smirks at me, his smile a little bit lopsided due to the swelling on part of his lip. "I just had an idea for a new tattoo. I thought you'd want to come," he tells me with a shrug. Suddenly, his face lights up. "Hey, maybe you can get that tattoo that you told me about," he says excitedly.

But I'm already shaking my head. "I don't have the money for that right now," I admit to him, even though the idea of getting a tattoo does excite me. There's only one thing that I've ever thought I'd be willing to put permanently on my body, and it's a quote. My favorite quote in the world is "she believed she could, so she did." I've loved that quote long enough, and it has special enough meaning for my dreams for myself, that I know I won't get tired of it if I did ever put it on my body.

"How about I pay for it as an early birthday present?" he offers. "Come on, Princess. It will be fun to get something done together," he practically begs.

"My birthday isn't for six months," I remind him, knowing that he will still get me other presents even if he bought me this right now. I'm always uncomfortable when they spend money on me, because I don't have anything to offer in return.

"Princess, you have to do it." The fact that he looks better just thinking about the idea of us getting tattoos together is the only reason that I find myself agreeing to it.

"Okay," I reluctantly grumble, a small twinge of excitement building up inside me at the thought of doing this. We get out of the car and walk into the tattoo shop. It's actually quite full, considering the time of night. This must be where Tanner had gotten at least some of his tattoos, because the employees all seem to know him. They also don't seem perturbed about his injuries, and I'm not sure what that means.

One guy, a skinny redhead with gauges in both ears and who is covered in brightly colored tattoos, walks over to us. He exchanges that handshake that all guys seem to somehow know with Tanner. "Hey, man, what's up? Haven't seen you in here for a while," he tells Tanner. The redhead looks over at me curiously, wiping his eyes up and down me appreciatively for a second, before turning back to Tanner.

"Mine," Tanner says casually, but the warning in his voice is easy to hear. I flush. What did that mean, that I was his?

The redhead holds up his hands in mock defensiveness. "I get it man, but you can't blame me for looking," he says.

Tanner rolls his eyes. "Princess, this idiot's name is Grant," he tells me. "He's done most of my tattoos."

"You do great work," I comment lamely, both guys smirking at my awkwardness.

"What are you looking for today?" Grant asks Tanner when they're done torturing me.

"I have a design in mind," Tanner says mysteriously. "But she needs to go first before she chickens out," he says, pointing at me.

"You're getting your first one?" Grant asks, looking like he's salivating at the thought of it.

"Apparently," I murmur, and Grant grins wickedly. "Once you start you won't be able to stop. It's an addiction," he tells me.

"We'll see if I can make it through one before we talk about not being able to stop," I tell him with a laugh.

Grant leads us to his station, which I'm excited to see is hidden from view of the rest of the shop behind a partition. "I don't like people watching me work," he explains as he gestures for me to hop up onto a leather chair that looks vaguely like the kind a dentist uses.

"Okay, what you got for me?" he asks, staring at me eagerly. I pull up the quote on my phone. I had found a picture on Pinterest a few months ago that had the quote in a font that I really liked.

"I dig it," he says. "Email that to me so I can print it out." After giving me his email address, he wanders off to pick up the picture from the computer in the back.

"You don't have to do this," Tanner says suddenly, looking a little chagrined.

"I want to," I tell him honestly. "Sometimes, I just need to be pushed into doing things that I want. It's hard for me to think I deserve things that I want," I admit to him, immediately feeling stupid for even saying that.

"I get that," he says, staring at me intensely, and I can see that he actually does. "We're more alike than I first thought, you and I," he murmurs, looking thoughtful...and conflicted. "What secrets do you have, Ariana Kent?" he asks.

Before I can utter a response, Grant's back, waving the paper in front of him like he's won an award.

"It's going to look great," he says reassuringly, since I'm sure my face is starting to display the panic I'm beginning to feel. "So, where are we putting this?" he asks, and my mind goes blank. I immediately think of those grandmas who have made the unfortunate decision when they were younger to put tattoos in places that stretched badly over time. It was not an attractive thing when a rose tattoo ended up resembling a twisted smiley face because the skin had become so wrinkled.

"Okay, I can give you some advice if you'd like," Grant says when I haven't come up with anything. I nod eagerly. "Are you wanting to have it where someone can see it all the time, or do you want it easily hidden, like if you have a job that frowns upon tattoos."

"Hidden," I answer quickly, knowing that I want the option of showing it or not.

"There's really only one place on a woman's body that doesn't stretch much if they get pregnant or if they just gain weight in general. So, I usually suggest that my female clients put their quote tattoos there, if it's not going someplace like their inner wrist or somewhere like that. Can you lift your arm for me?" he asks.

I lift my left arm up, and he gently taps the area on my rib cage, about five inches from the bottom of my armpit. "This is where I usually suggest. It's one of the last places that people seem to gain weight, so your tattoo should maintain its shape."

He was talking about weight and pregnancy an awful lot, but I guess it made sense. A moment of blind panic passes over me as I think about having kids. That was what usually happened to girls who came from my trailer park, though. I knew of at least three from our class that dropped out to have kids just in the past year.

I shiver at the thought of bringing a child into the hell I called my life.

"That sounds good," I tell Grant, looking at Tanner to see what he thinks. He actually doesn't look too happy at the moment.

"Do you have some sort of blanket she can put over the front of her?" Tanner asks, brushing his hair out of his face with a frown. It's been a while since he got a haircut.

Grant smirks at him. "I'm sure we can arrange something like that," he tells him in a knowing tone. I swear, Tanner growls in response to Grant's teasing.

I understand why Tanner was worried when I have to pull up my shirt and unclasp the back of my bra. Grant gives me a blanket to put over the front of me, but it's still a little bit awkward to have this much skin showing in front of both Grant and Tanner. I'm just grateful that the rest of the shop can't see me too. Tanner's eyes keep darting to the skin that's showing, and by the heated look in them, he seems to like the view.

Grant places the design he printed out on my skin and explains that it would leave an outline on my skin that he will then trace over with the tattoo gun to make sure that the design is perfect when he actually uses the tattoo gun. After doing the trace, I watch as Grant makes the ink. I was just going with black. The font I found was very thin and dainty, and I didn't think that a white tattoo would look very good.

I start to freak out when he turns the tattoo gun on. It's so loud that I'm a little afraid that he actually turned on a buzz saw and I'm about to die. Tanner must've seen the beads of sweat that are starting to develop on my forehead, because he walks over and takes my hand, giving me a reassuring squeeze.

"This is going to look so fucking hot," he tells me reassuringly, his eyes almost ravenous at this point.

Of course, I blush at that comment.

It takes a lot for me not to scream when the tattoo gun touches my skin. It feels like I'm being stabbed over and over again, and I can't believe that people actually get addicted to this sort of thing and want more.

"You're doing so good, Princess," Tanner says as he avidly watches Grant work.

Eventually, it stops hurting as much, or my skin just becomes a little numb to the pain. The feeling is almost like I'm having an out of body experience while Grant works, and I'm flying above my body as it happens. Maybe this feeling is what brings people back time and time again.

The feeling of being free.

When it's over, I'm surprised to see that only twenty minutes have passed. "I'm done already?" I ask, and Grant and Tanner both chuckle.

"Do you want to see it?" Grant asks, and I nod nervously, all of a sudden envisioning a scenario where he actually tattooed something ridiculous on me, like a naked woman or something like that.

Grant holds up a mirror, and I let out a little squeal. It's perfect. It's exactly like the picture I had found, and it was just the right size. I loved it.

Grant puts some kind of Vaseline type stuff on it and then he tapes it up and gives me the aftercare instructions. And then, it's Tanner's turn.

"This one is going on my back, left side," he says to Grant, winking at me as he does so as if he's picked the left side to match me. Thinking about it though, I realize that I've only seen tattoos on that side. I wonder what that's all about.

"Are you okay with being here for awhile, Princess?" Tanner asks, and I nod, ignoring the fact that I have school tomorrow, something I have no plans of skipping since graduation might be my only ticket out of here.

"I want an angel wing," he tells Grant. "Something like this," he says, pulling an image up on his phone and showing him. Grant looks at it admiringly. "That's going to hurt like a bitch," he tells him, but Tanner just grins as if the idea of pain delights him.

"Do you want that exact thing or do you want me to sketch something up?" Grant asks, and Tanner gives him a "what do you think" kind of look.

Grant rolls his eyes and disappears in the back without another word.

"I need a smoke," Tanner says abruptly, and disappears behind the partition.

Tanner comes back fifteen minutes later smelling of tobacco and him. He looks more relaxed than he did before he left, and I wonder what demon he had to chase out of his head this time.

Grant's back shortly after Tanner's return with the angel wing drawing that Tanner requested. But if it's an angel wing, it definitely belongs to a fallen one. And it fits Tanner perfectly. Something about the design is dark and broken. This wing wasn't built from heaven's light. This wing came from pain. It's weird how you can see all of that just in a drawing, but the proof is right in front of my face.

Somehow, it's not as shocking as it should be when Tanner casually lifts his shirt up, and I see that his back is covered with scars, as if someone's cut him over and over again until the skin just gave up on the idea of regenerating itself. There's a fresh set of lashes on the left side that looks like it's just started to scab over.

"Holy shit," Grant spits out, sounding sick at the sight. But Tanner doesn't pay any attention to his reaction, his focus is on me. There's a challenge in his gaze, as if he's daring me to run away at the sight or worse...ask him what happened.

I keep my face blank, even though I'm crying inside. I'm only faintly aware of Tanner and Grant arguing over the fact that Tanner wants Grant to tattoo over his injured skin. Grant's either an idiot or he's just known Tanner long enough to know that he would just go somewhere else to get it done if he has to, because he gives in. Tanner lays down on his stomach, his face turned towards me, and Grant begins.

"You're going to have to come in a few days for me to finish this. You know I can't do it all tonight," Grant says once he gets going, but Tanner doesn't respond. Hours pass, and Tanner's silver gaze doesn't stray from mine.

It's like we're in our own little world. As the hours pass, Tanner lets me see his pain, and I give him a glimpse of mine. And I know that when we're done here that something will have irrevocably changed between us. Something that we never will be able to go back from. My heart recognizes him in this moment as someone who can understand me like maybe no one else can.

His heart calls to me like it has from the beginning, and I've never wanted to answer it more.

Tanner never flinches or shows any sign that he's experiencing pain, and I guess by his existing injuries, that makes sense. Tanner's used to physical injuries, it's the emotional ones he has trouble dealing with.

Grant's dead on his feet when he's finally finished, muttering something about Tanner owing him his first born child after this. I can see the pride over his work emanating from him, though. And he should be proud. It's almost like he's transformed Tanner over the last few hours, and Tanner has become something bigger...something more.

Tanner's lips purse as he examines the tattoo in the mirror, as if he recognizes the change but doesn't know what to think of it. He'll have to come in to finish the shading soon but the work that has been done is spectacular.

Tanner pays and claps Grant on the back before slipping

him a tip that makes me almost faint at how much it is.

We head outside to where the sun is starting to appear in this sky, and I know that I'm going to be exhausted today at school. But I also know that the tiredness will be worth it.

We drive through a Starbucks before Tanner heads to school, even though we've still got an hour before it begins. He parks in the mostly empty parking lot, and then we just stare at each other. When his lips finally meet mine softly, it's like I'm coming home. His hand moves to my waist, and he pulls me closer while simultaneously coaxing my lips open. I don't resist, not even for a moment. Before I realize it, my hands find his hair, and I dig my fingers in, keeping him close. His tongue traces the opening of my lips, and his grip tightens on my waist. This kiss is different. It's just as intoxicating as the others, but it's different. It's a sleepy kiss, not a kiss of two people getting to know each other, but rather, a kiss of reverence. The level of feeling in this kiss is deep, heady, and confident. My heart beats double time, and I feel completely and utterly powerless.

Panic sets in a moment later, and I pull away, resting my forehead on his shoulder. My breathing is urgent and fractured, and I squeeze my eyes shut, suddenly terrified of what it all means. I've now kissed Jesse, Jensen, and Tanner. Tanner's hand runs over my hair and down my back soothingly. What. The. Hell. One tattoo, and my self-control is MIA; I can't calm down. A million thoughts rush through my head, fighting their way to materialize on my lips. I push them down and pull away from Tanner, giving him what I hope isn't a shaky smile. "Thank you for last night," I tell him. His eyes search mine. He knows something just shifted within me but he doesn't press.

"I think you already said that about a million times."

I laugh. "Right. Well, thanks again." He nods and leans back, tucking his hands in his lap like he's having to prevent himself from touching me. "My pleasure, Princess."

10
NOW

ARIANA

I'm still sitting on the couch, talking with Amberlie when Clark appears. We're surrounded by bodyguards, but Clark just ignores their presence as he sidles up to us.

"Ariana," he says. "It's good to see you."

I smile up at him. "Thanks for all the work you've been doing for the guys. I don't know what they would have done if you hadn't been able to step in after everything that happened."

He shrugs. "It's my job," he says simply, but I know that the work he's done has been over and beyond what an agent usually does.

"How have you been feeling?" he asks, staring at me intently. "Has that doctor I sent you helped?"

"I went for the first time today. I'm a work in progress," I respond honestly. There's not really a point in trying to lie to him. I'm sure he's been given at least some updates from the guys, or he's at least noticed the strange tension between the four of us.

"I have a proposition for you that I think you'll be excited about," said Clark, staring at me intently. "Hopefully, you're ready for it."

A tiny prickle starts to creep up along my spine, for some reason, I know that whatever is going to come out of his mouth is going to be big. I can see Amberlie lean forward excitedly out of the corner of my eye.

"Okay," I tell him a little unsteadily.

"I recorded a couple of sessions of you jamming with the guys on the bus during the tour," he admits to me, not indicating he feels bad about it at all. "I've shown it to the label. And Ari, they like what they've seen. Actually...they fucking love what they've seen. And they'd like to bring you into the studio and talk about a contract," he tells me, opening up a folder that I've just noticed he's holding. He says all of this casually, like he's hasn't dropped the biggest news I've ever received on me.

All the breath has left my body. He has to be joking. Good things like this don't happen to me. "Is this for real?" I whisper. "Did the guys put you up to this?" I ask, looking around to see where they were. They were still in sound check apparently, because they are nowhere to be found.

"Ariana, this has nothing to do with them. You have talent all on your own, that doesn't depend on the Sound of Us," he tells me calmly, as if he expected that question. I nervously push my hair behind my ear and peek at Amberlie's reaction. She looks like she's about to explode with excitement while she mouths to me a silent "oh my gosh." Her over the top reaction helps me calm down some, and I turn my attention back to Clark.

Clark hands me documents out of the folder. My eyes widen as I start to skim over them. "I've looked over the offer myself, and it looks better than normal for a brand-new artist. But I do advise you to have a lawyer look over the contract as well," he tells me as he points out some features of the contract that I wouldn't have noticed.

"I'm sure the guys have someone that can look over it," I mutter as my eyes skim over the second page.

He clears his throat. "Actually, I think it would be good for you to get your own lawyer. I'd like to be your agent and manager, if you're willing. I really believe in you. But I think that it's best for your career if you have separation. Getting to where you're known for your talent and not as the girlfriend of the hottest band around will be crucial for you succeeding in this business," he tells me slowly, obviously weighing his words since the guys would freak out if they heard him say something like this. I'm freaking out hearing him say it.

I open my mouth to object, but then close it. What he's saying does make sense. The tabloids right now are full of questions about who I am, and speculation on if I was dating all of them. How was I ever going to be taken seriously if they were so focused on me as the object of the guys' affection, rather than a burgeoning new talent? Not that I really believed I would be thought of as that. This didn't seem real. This couldn't be real.

"Still, I think it would be wise for us to use that song that you and Jensen wrote as your first single to kind of introduce you to the stage. But after that, I think you should introduce some of the songs that you've written," he tells me. I look at him in surprise. Before I can say anything, he interjects. "Don't try to say that you don't have spirals full of songs you've written. I've seen you feverishly writing by yourself whenever you get a free moment. I know that those notebooks aren't just filled with journals and quotes," he tells me, cracking a grin.

I nod reluctantly, my face blushing with heat at the idea of the world hearing anything that I've written. More than likely, they would hear some of the songs and reject it right away as being total crap. Stuff that I've written with the guys is much better than any of that.

"We're also going to work on your confidence," he tells

me, watching me closely. "You need to believe that this is happening to you- because of you and not because of them," he tells me seriously. "You'll be eaten alive if you can't recognize your own talent. There's always going to be naysayers saying crap. I can't believe in you for you," he tells me.

I know he's right. It's something that has been haunting me for a while. Like Dr. Mayfield said, I'm like a ship lost at sea. For so long, my identity depended on them. That wasn't sustainable.

Clark pulls out another piece of paper. "This is the contract that would allow me to be your agent and manager. As you can see, I'll only be taking a small percentage at first. That will give me the chance to prove to you that I believe in you and that I can help you be successful in this industry," he tells me.

I can't believe this still, yet everything in me is desperate for this to be true and not a cruel prank. The artists he manages are some of the biggest in the world. It's an honor for him to even want to work with me. "When was the last time, besides the guys that you even started out with a new artist?" I ask as an unsavory thought hit me. I really needed to be sure that his interest didn't have anything to do with wanting to get between the sheets with me. I'm pretty sure my heart would be broken if that was the case.

His face softens. "Ariana, I go with my gut when I make decisions, and I'm rarely wrong. In fact, I've never had an artist fail since my career began. I know when someone has talent. And that someone in this case is you." He stands up from the couch and brushes off his slacks. "Why don't you take a few days to think it over? The label would like to get you into a studio as soon as possible, but I understand that this is a major decision for you. You have my number, text me or call me if you have a question and we can get this started." I nod numbly.

He begins to walk away, and then stops and turns around.

"Ariana, you know they're not gonna like this. But you need to make this decision for yourself," he tells me seriously. He waits until I've nodded my agreement before walking away again.

He's right. The guys will have a problem with this. Not because they don't want me to be someone, but I think they're so worried about my safety after everything that they aren't exactly thinking of me in terms of what would make me happy. They were thinking in terms of what would be the safest, and in this case, those two things would appear to them to be directly conflicting with one another.

I was sure that if it came down to it, I could get a bodyguard or even a couple of bodyguards. I peer at the number again that the record label is agreeing to pay me in the contract, and I can't help but smile widely. I would be able to afford my own bodyguards if it came down to it.

The other problem of course, was that I'm still a wreck. What would I do if there was a loud sound while I was performing on stage, and I freaked out? That would shoot my chances of success down before I even began if I couldn't get ahold of myself. Of course, that made me think of Dr. Mayfield's words today, that she thought my reactions had more to do with my lack of purpose and my fear of life in general than it did over what happened with Gentry. Maybe with work, I could do this. Maybe this would be the "doing something for me" that she talked about.

Maybe this could be the start of me.

"Pinch me," I tell Amberlie breathlessly, and she giggles as she does so. "Is the contract still in my hand?" I ask her, squeezing my eyes closed with wonder.

"Are the guys really going to be upset?" she asks, and I shrug, not wanting to talk right now about everything that had been happening with them.

"I'm sure it will be fine. I just have to decide if it's something that I want to do," I tell her.

She screeches so loud that I'm afraid that my eardrum is going to pop. "Ariana Kent, don't make me punch you. This is a once in a lifetime opportunity sweetheart. You may not have told me anything yet, but I know that the last few years couldn't have been good to you with the way you cut me off. This is your good thing," she tells me.

But she's wrong. No matter what she says, Clark says, or Dr. Mayfield says, I learned a long time ago that a love like ours is my good thing. And whatever I do, I can't lose that. I just have to hope that there's a path that can include my dreams and them.

I decide to wait to tell the guys about Clark's offer until after the show so I don't distract them. Even though I haven't admitted it to Amberlie, I am worried about their response.

My thoughts are interrupted when I'm suddenly picked up off the couch and Tanner's lips are against mine. I had almost forgotten about the fact that Tanner kisses me before every show. With everything that has been happening between us, I guess I was actively trying not to think about it, just in case I was disappointed and he skipped it this time.

He's gone after just a second, disappearing on stage to give the screaming masses what they're begging for, but just the one kiss gives me hope that everything is going to be okay.

I can barely sit still through the whole concert. My thoughts are complicated, made worse because they're slightly off tonight. The tension of the past few months has bled out onto the stage and into the music, and even though they still sound amazing, there's a certain something that's lacking that anyone who was really a fan would recognize.

The guys, for their part, don't seem to be as interested in the performance as they should be. Instead, they keep shooting me looks, either from concern about my safety or because they can tell I'm distracted. Or maybe it's a little bit of both.

I try to enjoy the show, especially because Amberlie hasn't seen them since they made it big, and she seems to be having the time of her life.

When the band rushes backstage after the concert without doing an encore, I realize just how badly I've been doing at hiding that something is going on.

Jensen grabs my arm and drags me towards his dressing room, Tanner and Jesse following close behind. "I'll just wait right here," Amberlie yells behind us worriedly.

Jensen just shoots her a thumbs up before slamming the door behind all of us. They're all crowded around me. "What's going on? Is everything alright?" Jensen asks worriedly. I'm temporarily distracted by the play of his muscles as he crosses his arms in front of his chest, but the thought of my new opportunity brings me back to the present quickly.

"I talked to Clark while you guys were in sound check, and he had something exciting to tell me," I begin carefully, fiddling nervously with a ring on my hand.

"Did he have updates on Gentry?" Tanner interjects, and my heart sinks. This, this is why this opportunity is so good. Maybe it'll help us move past worrying about Gentry every second.

"No, this has nothing to do with that. Clark took recordings of some of our sessions on the bus, and your record label loved them," I tell him excitedly. I expect them to start showing interest, but all three of them are carefully blank. Okay then. "Clark said that they love my voice, and they offered me a contract," I continue, pulling the papers out of my purse that I haven't been able to set down. "They want me to start recording some songs right away. Clark felt the one that you and I had written might be good for a single," I tell Jensen, who's still not showing any emotion. "I looked through the documents, but of course I'm not an expert. Clark wants me to get a lawyer to look after them. But the terms seem amazing from what I know. And Clark wants to be my manager, can you believe that? He's even doing it a lower percentage to start out with," I tell them, still expecting some kind of reaction.

"It seems too good to be true, but the documents outline everything…" My voice trails off as I realize that the guys don't seem happy with this development, and the more I talk, the worse the feeling in the room seems to get.

Jesse has taken the contract from me and is skimming through it, his face looking more annoyed the farther down the page he gets. But now I'm getting annoyed at their reaction. Haven't I been happy with them for every success that they've had in their lives, even the one that left me alone in hell? At least if I'm away from them they'll have each other. When they left, I had no one.

I take a deep breath, knowing that that wasn't a fair assessment of the situation. They had no idea what my life was going to be like once they left because I never told them. We weren't like that anymore. All our cards were on the table.

"What do you guys think?" I finally say. Only silence answers me. Jesse's still reading through the contract, Tanner's staring at me still numbly, and Jensen looks like he's about to burst.

Jensen takes a deep breath. "I don't know that this is the best time to be doing something like that," he finally says carefully. I just look at him in shock. I knew that there would be mixed feelings about this, but I didn't expect them to just not want me to take the opportunity at all.

"Jensen, you can't possibly mean that," I respond shakily. But he doesn't take back his statement. And looking at Jesse, who has now finished reading over the contract, and Tanner, who still is just staring at me, I know that they all feel the same way.

I laugh bitterly. "Look, if this is about Gentry, I'm sure that precautions can be made. If I stay hidden forever, that's just letting him win. I was already locked inside his cage for five years, I'm not about to let him do that to me again." It's an echo of words I've already told them...but that was before I was shot.

"I can't be around you all right now," I finally say before walking to the door. I stop before opening it and look back at them over my shoulder. "I'm doing this, and you're just going to have to get on board," I say before opening the door and slamming it shut behind me.

A part of me worries that I've just slammed the door on us.

11
NOW

ARIANA

Amberlie left the next morning. We should have been catching up for lost time, but after my disagreement with the guys, I wasn't up to it. Instead, we endured a silent car ride back to Jesse's mansion with my bodyguards while the guys signed autographs and did a meet and greet. Amberlie didn't push me to tell her what was going on, and I was grateful for that. We watched a movie in the mansion's theater room and binged on bad for you food.

It was nice to have a friend.

I rode with her to the airport, and we both cried as she got out of the car to go inside. But at least now we could talk on the phone. I knew someday she would demand answers, they all would, but I was grateful that day wasn't today.

The mansion was silent when I got back, and I didn't look for anyone, still upset about how the conversation went the night before. After hiding out watching more trashy reality television, I finally decided to leave my self-imposed solitude and go find them.

I find Tanner in one of the lounges, sitting in the dark with nothing but the light from the moon and the lit-up city illuminating him. He's sipping his favorite whiskey as he stares out at the California skyline.

"What are you doing in here, baby?" I joke with him, knowing he hates when I call him that.

But all I'm met with is silence. I sigh and take a seat next to him.

"It's only for a few months, Tanner," I tell him. "And we'll see each other throughout the tour."

"It's only a few months now," he says. "But eventually it will be half a year...then a whole year. Just you wait. Your music is going to go crazy on the airwaves. This will be just the beginning." His voice is a mix of pride and anger.

"Why is it so hard for you all to be happy for me? I supported your dreams, your lives...your everything since I met you. Why can't you do that for me now?"

"I am happy for you," he says in a voice that sounds as far from happy as possible. "But I don't understand why we can't do this together. We used to be a good thing, Princess. What happens when this becomes your good thing or someone else that you meet out there on the road becomes your good thing?"

"I'm not a cheater," I tell him staunchly, a tiny flicker in my head reminding me that I also slept with his two best friends regularly.

"I know you're not a cheater, Ari," he says, shaking his head.

"And you all are still my good thing. My very best thing," I tell him, stroking his hair softly, soothingly.

Like he did most times I touched him, he leaned into me, soaking in the love I was offering him.

I pull away after a moment and take his face in both my hands, so that he can't look away from me. "Remember that night on the beach when you told me you were gonna make it out of our town?" I asked.

"Yes," Tanner responded hoarsely, his eyes glued to mine.

"Well, I made that same vow. I just never admitted it out loud because I was afraid of failing."

"Okay, but we both made it out. We're here now, aren't we?" he asks, confused.

I shake my head. "You see, the thing is, Tanner, I never really got out of there. And the more I depend on you, the more I stay scared of Gentry and my past...the more it becomes clear to me that I'm still stuck there, and I'm always going to be stuck there, unless I can do something for myself. And, Tanner," I continue, my voice breaking with emotion. "I want to get out of there more than anything."

There's a long silence where we just stare at each other, but I know that he understands now. He understands me and why this opportunity has nothing to do with becoming rich and famous, or any of the other things that motivate most people trying to get their music out into the world. This is about me proving something to myself. That I'm not the trailer park girl from the wrong side of the tracks who happened to get lucky by meeting three boys who made it big. I think that part of me has always thought that I wasn't good enough for them. Maybe that's why it was so easy for me to break contact with them when my life went to shit after they left. I had a feeling that if I could do this, if I could prove to myself that I was somebody without them, then our relationship would be stronger than ever. We just had to make it through the journey first.

He pulls me to him and lays a gentle kiss on my lips that says everything he hadn't said out loud. "I love you, Ariana Kent. That's never going to change," he swears fiercely as he pulls away. "I never want to lose you."

My response is to nip his bottom lip, sucking it into my mouth. An instant bolt strikes me down low, and I'm aching for him. My teeth follow his racing pulse down his neck to the sensitive point just above his collarbone. Stopping, I rest my head there and take a deep breath, murmuring into his skin, "I don't know how to ease your fear. But I'm here. I will always be here for you, Tanner." I find his eyes and say, "Always. I will give you whatever you need."

"I need you, whole and healthy and with me."

"I am with you. We'll stumble every once in a while, but I promise you we'll never fall." I kiss him, and he licks my lips.

"We will never be broken," I whisper.

I just hope that I'm right.

I couldn't really believe that this was my life as our car-that the label sent-drives us to the recording studio. We could have driven ourselves but I guess Clark wanted to make sure that I actually made it to the studio, and that I wasn't delayed by the guys.

There's a part of me that can't help but think about how this was the way it was supposed to be all along, since this is the same studio that the guys were sent to when they got their start as well. If things had been different, I would have already been here and known exactly what it was like. It's like we're rewriting history, just five and a half years later.

Jesse winks at me as we drive when he sees my excited face. I'm sure I look like a kid in a candy store. Even Jensen's face is softened when he sees how thrilled I am with this development. We used to talk about our dreams, and he knows how much this means to me, even if he's scared of me being away from them.

I have my writing notebook with me, and I'm suddenly afraid of what the record label's going to think about everything that's inside of it. A lot of the songs I wrote with Jensen and the others, but some of them I wrote by myself. And I've only shown the guys some of them. But it's important to me that something that came from just me ends up on this record.

I want this to feel somewhat like I earned it, and not just that I've managed to ride on their coattails once again.

I had never actually been in a recording studio before, so my nerves are going haywire as we step into the main lobby. Tanner sent a text to me telling me he would meet me here a little later, so it's just Jesse and Jensen with me as we walk in. Jesse and Jensen greet an unkempt guy, who stands behind a fancy looking counter playing a video game on his phone. "Hey, man." The three shake hands.

"Aren't you guys still on tour? I thought it would be a while before a new album," he says to the guys.

"We're actually here for Ariana," says Jensen, gesturing to me.

The guy's eyes widen as he looks me up and down. "You're Ariana? The studio has been buzzing about you for a while," he says admiringly. "They let me listen to one of the recordings of you and it was epic."

I couldn't help but blush at his words. It was nice to hear someone outside of the guys say that I had talent. In the corner of my mind, I always wondered if they were nice about my singing because they were sleeping with me, or if I was actually good. I even had doubts about Clark's intentions, although they were starting to seem better and better every day.

Obviously, my self-confidence was a work in progress.

"Well, we better get started. Is everyone already back there?" asks Jesse before my inability to speak can get awkward.

"Sure are," the guy responds. "They've been there for a few days working on some stuff. Go on back...Studio D." He buzzes open a heavy-looking door and allows us to pass. I trail behind Jesse and Jensen as they lead me down a hallway, past a few rooms that are filled to the brim with instruments, to a large kitchen. In a way, it doesn't feel too overwhelming until we step out the back door on to a wood patio surrounded by lush gardens and tropical palm trees. There are four small houses out here that I assume are the individual recording studios. I follow the guys to the deck outside of Studio D where a guy is lounging by a stone table.

"You're here," a hazel eyed guy wearing a beat up red baseball cap greets us, grinning. "What's new?" he asks Jesse and Jensen, his eyes intent on me, though.

"Not much, Chris. Just ready to see what you guys have come up with," Jensen answers, shaking his hand at the same time he wraps his other arm around me possessively.

"This must be Ariana," Chris says excitedly, letting go of Jensen's hand quickly and offering it to me. "I'm one of your technicians," he tells me. "Are you ready for this? It's really a pleasure to get to work with you," said Chris admiringly. "I've listened to the recordings from Clark about a million times. You don't see talent like yours very often."

It's hard for me to form words as my tongue suddenly seems to weigh five thousand pounds from my nerves.

"A little nervous?" he asks, nodding his head understandingly. "Don't be. We're putting together epic shit today," he says, and I can't help but laugh at his enthusiasm. Chris is eyeing me appreciatively, and I feel the guys stiffen beside me. Oh, dear. Chris is attractive in that boy next door kind of way, but he can't hold a candle to my guys. I reach out and grab both Jensen's and Jesse's hands after I shake Chris's, trying to comfort them. It was a little funny to see the tables turned. After all, I've been dealing with girls not only smiling at them, but also trying to get in their pants ever since I first met them.

Clark told me that he'd already sent along some of the songs that Jensen and I had written together, and Chris and a few others have been coming up with some tracks to show us for us to record today.

"Should we get to work?" barks Jensen in an annoyed

voice and Chris shoots him a wry look, as it was easy to hear the jealousy in Jensen's voice.

Chris holds my gaze for a second longer, before finally releasing it and taking a step away from me. "We've been working on that song that Clark sent over, and I think it's ready to lay down some vocals. We got the scratch track done a few days ago and recorded the rest of the instruments yesterday," he says walking towards the sound booth. I have no idea what he means by scratch track, and the nervousness I'm feeling ramps up. However, when we follow him inside and I see the room that I've only imagined, my nerves flee and are replaced by chills of excitement.

Chris gestures us to sit on a worn, brown leather couch behind the sound booth. He begins to fiddle with some buttons over where the rest of the sound engineers have set themselves up. A few buttons later, and a catchy beat starts to come on. It's a pop song, but there's elements of rock laced throughout it, setting it apart from the songs that you usually hear on the radio. It's very close to what I envisioned when Jensen and I wrote the song. I immediately start to sing the words in my head along with the track. I can see Jensen's reluctant pleasure at how good it sounds as well. It's outside my realm to truly fathom that this is really happening, or everything else that has happened in the last few days. I feel like I'm either dreaming or having some sort of out of body experience. All I can hope is that I don't wake up.

After it finishes, Chris asks if we're ready. I'm supposed to be singing this song with Tanner, but he still hasn't gotten here, and I'm starting to get upset when I realize that Tanner is already thirty minutes late. He knows how much this means to me, and that the studio has only given us a few weeks to get this done. I thought after our conversation the other night that he would be taking this seriously for me.

As if he read my mind, Jesse pulls out his phone and presses Tanner's number. "You're late," he snaps at him, sounding very un-Jesse like. "You're screwing this up for us, man," he says. Jesse listens for one more minute and then hangs up. "Tanner will be here soon," he says, but I can tell that whatever Tanner said didn't make him happy.

Another thirty minutes pass before Tanner shows up. Luckily, Jensen and Jesse had some suggestions for the track that they worked on implementing with Chris, so it's not a total waste of time.

My eyes widen when Tanner walks into the room. He's wearing a stained shirt that has seen better days, his hair is a greasy mess, and his eyes are blood-shot. To top off the look, he's sporting a purpling eye. Everyone in the room goes silent as we look at the train wreck in front of us. Jesse and Jensen look like they are going to kill him.

"Are you okay?" I ask quietly, examining his gaunt features. I hadn't noticed how much weight he has lost over the last few months since I was shot. He's still beautiful, but he doesn't look like he's doing well.

"I'm great," he tells me, pulling me in for a kiss that leaves me breathless, despite my frustration with his tardiness and the fact that he clearly isn't taking care of himself. I force myself to break the kiss after it starts to become heated.

"What happened to your eye?"

He waves my concern away. "I just went out with some friends last night and got into a little fight at a bar. Not a big deal."

I go to open my mouth, but he presses his lips over mine again, cutting me off. He pulls away after he feels my body go slack. "Let's record your kick-ass song, rockstar," he teases me, and I decide to drop the issue for now.

Jensen hands us the lyric pages, muttering something scathing to Tanner that I can't make out. Tanner just ignores him and guides me into the booth, where two microphones have been set up. He hands me a set of headphones before placing his on. Giving me a reassuring grin, he gives Chris a thumbs up, and the music starts playing.

My voice is shaky from nerves when I first start, and we have to restart a few times before I level out and sound normal. Despite Tanner's obviously rough night, he sounds amazing, and I marvel at the way our voices blend together. I almost forget to sing at one point because of the way he's looking at me, like he's falling more in love with me as we stand there. The song weaves around us, spinning magic into the air. I forget where we are. It's just Tanner and me in this moment. The last note fades, and there's a short silence before we hear clapping. I look over and see that Clark has stepped into the room. I can almost see the dollar signs in his eyes.

We step out of the booth to get the reaction from the others. "You sounded amazing, baby," says Jensen, lifting me in the air with a small whoop. I grin at him, probably looking a bit crazy as I'm experiencing that high that the guys always get when they perform, even though I'm not performing for anyone. I look to Jesse to see his reaction and see that he's talking to Chris, gesturing with his hands emphatically.

"Jesse?" I ask.

"There's something off with the bass. It needs to be more active," he tells Chris, who purses his lips as he thinks about it.

"There's nothing wrong with the bass," snaps Tanner, sounding agitated. "It's good enough how it is."

"Do you want it to be just fine for Ariana?" Jesse snaps back. "Good enough isn't good enough. This is Ari's first single. It has to be perfect."

"Here we go." Jensen groans, sitting down on the couch with a sigh. "They're always like this," he tells me, since I'm sure I look worried at the way they are talking to one another. "They will argue for a bit, and then Tanner will eventually meet Jesse halfway and then it will go on and on."

"Let's listen back," Jensen calls out to Chris, who nods.

Chris punches some buttons and music fills the room. I almost jump when I hear my voice, not believing that it's actually me that sounds that good. Everyone in the room listens, intent, to the entire song.

"One more time, please." Tanner gestures to Chris when the song is finished. Halfway through, he holds up his hand. "Stop! Play that part again?" Chris does as directed.

"See? Right there. Listen," Jesse says. "Wouldn't it sound better if the bass picked up here?" He picks up a bass laying against the wall and starts to play along with the song. I do like the bass, but I actually think that it's the drum that needs to pick up more here. I also realize that there's a few spots in the song that would sound better if I went up an octave.

I startle when Clark starts talking to me in a low voice, and I realize that he's standing right next to me. "Don't forget this is your song, for your album, Ariana. They may be contributing, but it's you on the line and not them. If you have an opinion, you need to speak up."

I nod, realizing that he's right. "I think we actually need more drums through this section, and more bass in the chorus," I announce. My voice comes out soft at first, and Jesse and Tanner don't hear me. Jensen gives me a little nudge, and I repeat it louder.

Jesse and Tanner both turn to me, looking chagrined. Evidently, they both realized that they were essentially taking over my song. Chris focuses his attention on me while Jensen moves to a set of drums. He starts beating a stronger rhythm over the song that Chris has replayed, and we all grin at each other when we hear how it sounds. Jesse adds more bass to the chorus, and I squeal a little bit when I hear it all coming together. The fact that I was right gives me confidence to tell everyone about my ideas for changes in the vocals. Tanner nods thoughtfully when he hears my ideas, and we get back into the vocal booth to re-record. Tanner and I smile as we move up an octave at the bridge, in agreement that the decision to change the chords was the right one. At one point Tanner is so excited about a verse of the song that I've just finished that he swoops in and gives me a spine tingling kiss. We have to restart, but I don't mind.

We take a break after we finish recording the vocals for the first single, and one of the studio's staff members brings in a tray of turkey wraps. Clark is in and out of the room, barking at Chris about when the final version of the song will be ready. Evidently, listening to the song has lit a fire under him. My hands shake slightly when I overhear him on the phone talking about potential media dates.

The guys stiffen when they hear what he's saying. I think they had been under the assumption that because the first single hadn't come out yet, that it would be a while before I would have obligations that would take me away from them. I kind of thought that too, but this song makes me excited to get started. I have that feeling like I'm standing on the edge of a precipice that's about to change everything.

I can't remember a day where I had more fun.

12
NOW

ARIANA

I walk into the studio two days later. We weren't supposed to have a recording session today, but I knew that the sound engineers would be laying down some tracks for other songs on the album. Chris and one of the other engineers, Michael I think was his name, were both fiddling on the sound board while drinking coffee.

Chris looks surprised to see me. "Ariana, I didn't think we had a session with you today. We're working on that track that you and Jesse put together."

I nod, feeling shy all of a sudden. I'm holding my song notebook tightly in my hand. "I have some other songs that I wanted you to look at," I tell him.

"Oh, that sounds great. Give me one more second, and then we can look them over."

I sit down on the couch, my hands slightly shaking as I look at the song that I was going to show him. It was one that I put together when I was married to Gentry. It was a song that talked about another life and what could've been. I knew that it would make the guys sad to hear it, and it was a song that felt deeply personal, so I wanted to work on it myself. Clark told them that I was going to be in a meeting with record people today, and that was how I'd been able to slip away. My two bodyguards were standing outside of the room, ever present.

Chris pulls up a stool in front of me. "Okay, what do you have for me?" he asks.

"I thought I would play it for you, if that's all right," I answer.

He chuckles. "You don't need to ask, this is your album, remember?" he tells me, shooting me an amused grin. I blush and walk over to the piano sitting in the corner. Setting up the notebook in front of me, I take a deep sigh, and I begin.

The words flow out of me. And even though I start off shaky once again as I had at the beginning of the first session, my voice quickly grows stronger. I thought at the time that I wrote this song, that it was a symbol of my weakness, my inability to grab hold of my dream. But now, as I sing it, I see it as something else. I see it as my anthem. Even four years into the worst marriage possible, I still let myself dream. I'd still let myself hope. There was still love laced throughout the words, and they were a testament to the fact that no matter how much time passed, I never stopped loving them. They had the same songs about me that they'd written while we were apart. The girl who wrote this hadn't been a nobody who had given up on life. She was still dreaming, still hoping. I could take pride in that.

The last notes fade away, and I open my eyes, realizing that I closed them as I was singing. There's silence, and then Michael and Chris both begin clapping loudly, elation written all over their faces.

"You wrote that?" Chris asks. I nod, shyness overcoming me once again, but I also feel an enormous sense of pride. Chris looks like his mind is already full of ideas for the song. "We're going to record you on the piano first and then lay down the rest of the instruments. But I think the piano should be the central base of the song," he tells me excitedly. I nod, thinking that was how I envisioned it as well.

We get to work right away. I'm glad that I get to see this song built from one instrument up as it feels like my baby. The other tracks that we recorded had basically been completed with just little touches here and there from the guys and I.

This song, I was a part of every step. Hours and hours pass as we work. It was all worth it. When I hear the song completed, tears gather in my eyes. I know it's going to be my favorite song on the album. And I can't wait for the guys to hear it.

Chris puts it on the flash drive so I can have the guys listen to it. The feeling in the room is joyful and light. It's amazing how cathartic it is to create this song, to turn my pain into art.

This is what I have always dreamed of doing.

I feel bad as I walk out of the recording studio, suddenly remembering my bodyguards are still out here. "I'm so sorry that took so long," I gush. "Were you able to get something to eat?" I ask, realizing how hungry I am after not taking a break. They nod politely.

"A girl brought us sandwiches, Miss Kent. No worries," Orlando tells me. He suddenly blushes. "I heard what you did in there. I have to say, that was pure magic," he tells me shyly. It's a little funny to see this mountain of a man acting so shy, but I really appreciate that he liked what he heard. The rooms were basically soundproof, so he would have heard only a little bit and was probably just being nice, but still, a compliment was a compliment. I'm working harder on accepting those better.

I'm practically desperate to get back to the mansion to show the guys. But as soon as I walk in through the front door, my excitement disappears. There's a heavy silence threaded throughout the house. And the deeper I venture in, the more it feels like I've found myself now attending a funeral.

I find the guys in one of the many living rooms. Tanner's drinking by the window, not an uncommon sight since I've been shot, but there's something about the heavy set of his shoulders that tells me whatever mood he is in is even worse than usual. Jesse is sitting on the couch, his face in his hands. And Jensen, Jensen is almost unrecognizable. He's standing by the bar cart, facing it, but there's broken glass and shredded pillows all around him. "What happened?" I ask worriedly, hesitantly taking a step towards him. My bodyguards are right behind me, and their eyes widen as they look around the room.

"I think you guys better leave," I tell them.

"Not until we find out that everything's okay," Orlando says seriously, obviously not liking the look of the room. I smile at him gently.

"I'm sure everything's fine. I just really need to be alone with them right now," I tell him, knowing that there wasn't a situation where the guys would ever present a danger to me.

They reluctantly leave, and as soon as they do, I want them to return. Just because maybe that would delay me hearing whatever they're about to tell me.

Jensen takes a deep breath and then turns around. I see that he's holding a stack of papers and my stomach starts clenching.

"What are these?" Jensen asks in a shaky voice. I take a step towards him until I'm close enough to his hands to see the papers he's holding. As soon as I see what's on them, my heart freezes. My breath literally just disappears from my body. I've done everything I can to make sure that those documents didn't see the light of day, especially after Gentry somehow got a hold of them.

I'm not sure what to do in the situation. Do I just tell them the worst part of me? Or do I keep doing what I've been doing since I've come back to them, and just ask them to give me time?

It feels like an important moment, the kind of moment that defines a relationship, that defines a life. Do I take the leap of faith?

"Don't lie to us, Ariana," Jesse suddenly barks, his voice so different from the gentle way he usually speaks to me. "Is this why you didn't come meet us in LA?"

Tears are gathering in his eyes as he looks at me. I'm not sure that he can actually handle the truth of those papers. I can't even handle what's in them, and they're about me.

"What do you have there?" I ask carefully, deciding I want a couple more seconds to gather myself.

Jensen gapes at me. "What do I have here? You know what I have here, Ariana. Gentry, or some other fucker who's also obsessed with you left this in a box by the front door. These appear to be your medical records. And they say…" His voice breaks and he tries to clear it before continuing. "They say that the reason that you didn't come to us all those years ago was because you were raped," he says brokenly.

He says what I've never been able to say out loud.

13
THEN

ARIANA

"I miss you," says Jesse through the phone, and I know he means it.

"What are you guys doing today?" I ask, fiddling with the frayed edges of my shirt.

"We'll be in the recording studio all day today, working with the label's producer. I can't fucking wait." I can hear how giddy he is through the phone, and it makes me smile, despite the fact that I've been in the worst possible mood since they left.

Only a few more weeks, I tell myself. But the weeks might as well be years for how slow time is passing.

"How's home been?" Jesse asks, his voice losing its happiness.

"It's fine," I lie. Lying over the phone is so incredibly easy.

The truth is that my Terry's drug use has amped up...and David has been creepier than ever. But I'm only a few weeks away from leaving. I don't need to worry the guys and distract them from what they're trying to do. I've handled this my whole life. I can handle it for a little while longer.

"Have you been staying in the library until it closes?" he asks.

"Yes. And I've been spending the night with Amberlie a lot," I tell him. But what I don't tell him is that Amberlie is at Nationals this week with our school's cheerleading team, and her house isn't an option this week.

But Jesse wouldn't know why that was such a problem.

I hear a voice in the background. "I'll be right there," Jesse yells to someone, and my heart clenches because even just talking to him on the phone makes me not feel so alone.

"I've got to go, pretty girl," he tells me, and I take a deep breath so I can keep the disappointment out of my voice.

"I'm so happy for you guys, Jesse," I respond. And I can practically hear how wide his smile is through the phone.

"See you soon," he tells me.

"Bye."

As I walk up to the dilapidated trailer that I call my home, it somehow looks even more menacing than usual, which is a tall task.

All the windows in the trailer are dark. For a moment, I think about going and sneaking into my room from the back window. But listening, it sounds like everyone's asleep. I cut my knee on a rusty nail the last time I had snuck in the back, and I wasn't eager to repeat that. I was still expecting I was gonna get some kind of disease from the who knows what on the nail.

Listening for another moment, I finally decide that it's safe. I pull out my key and insert it, and then open the door as quietly as possible. Every few seconds, I pause, listening in to see if I can hear anything. But the house is quiet. So quiet, I don't think that my mother and David are even here. I step inside and tiptoe down the hallway. Listening at their room through the closed door, I can't hear anything. They really must be out.

I walk a little farther down the hall until I get to my room.

It's pitch black, which is weird because I always leave a nightlight plugged in for when I come home late.

When you're surrounded by monsters like I am, you don't like the dark.

I go to turn on my light, and the door closes behind me.

I know who it is before I even turn around. He was specifically trying to be quiet before. And now that he's not, there's no hiding the sound of his excited breathing.

"I've been waiting for you, girl," he says to me.

"Well, I'm home. So you can leave now. I'd like to go to sleep. I have school tomorrow," I tell him.

"It's funny. Like you think you're too good for us now that you've been hanging out with those rich boys," he says as he slowly walks towards me. I inch my way backwards, looking around the room out of the corner of my eye to see if there's anything I can use to defend myself.

Because I have a feeling that I'm going to need to defend myself.

Unfortunately for me, I decided to clean my room this week, and there's nothing out that I can use.

"I don't think anything. You need to leave right now," I tell him, trying to keep the tremor and fear out of my voice. "Where's Terry?" I ask him, trying to keep my voice from sounding scared.

"Your mama is out paying off a little debt that she's incurred," he sneers. "Guess she shouldn't have had so much blow at Lexi's party last night."

I didn't know what "paying off" meant, since we had no money, but I could guess. And I could guess that David put her up to it. I shiver. I'm alone.

Trying to hide what I'm doing, I start to sneak my hand into my pocket to grab my phone so that I can dial for help. I'm not even sure who I can call, since everyone that I know is out of town, but surely there's someone.

He's on me before I can get the phone out of my pocket. "I

don't think so," he practically purrs, wrenching the phone out of my pocket and throwing it across the room. I stare at the shattered pieces in horror. This isn't happening. I'm supposed to be done with school in just a few weeks, and I'm supposed to be free, living out my dreams in LA with the guys.

I open my mouth to scream, but his sweaty, dirty hand covers my mouth before I can get more than a few decibels out. "Are you gonna be a good girl for me?" he asks as he begins to drag me toward my bed. I'm kicking and screaming, but it's like he's gotten superhuman strength overnight. By the look in his eyes, maybe he has. What is he on, bath salts?

"Please don't do this," I plead with him, trying to appeal to any sort of humanity that he holds within him.

"Don't act like you don't want this," he says with a sickening smile. "Just because you've gotten a taste of the rich boys doesn't mean that you're out of the trailer park. Them rich boys don't know how to satisfy a girl," he says as he reaches out and rips the top of my threadbare shirt.

I scramble to pull my top back up, but he doesn't let me. He's sweating even more right now, his pupils so wide that it looks like his eyes are actually black. He pushes me down on the bed, his hand returning to my mouth as I try to scream again. I'm kicking and thrashing until he pulls out a syringe.

"This should help you relax," he says as he stabs my arm with the needle. All I can hope for is that the needle is at least clean. As I drift off from whatever drug was in his syringe kicks in, I feel myself getting lighter. So light that it feels like I'm floating. I'm only faintly aware that the rest of my clothes are being torn off, that he's touching me in places that I've never been touched before.

I'm only faintly aware that I'm ruined.

He's gone by the time I come out of my stupor. I'm left with a dry throat and a headache so fierce that it feels like my brain is pounding its way out of my head. It takes all of my strength to push myself off the bed and pull on the scraps that are left of my shirt. I'm aching everywhere, and I can already tell that I've been violated.

There's blood on the bed around me.

I don't feel like myself, and in this moment, I think I've actually lost myself forever. I struggle to stand. Everything hurts so much that I know I have to see a doctor. I'm not even worried about reporting him, because the damage is already done. Punishing him doesn't make me whole, so it's not even a thought as I drag myself out of my room, down the hall, and out into the muggy night. I only have just enough strength to make it out the front door, and then I collapse at the foot of the stairs. As I lay there on the rocks and dirt that make up our yard, I wonder if this is what dying feels like.

I'm never going to see what they become, I whisper to myself softly.

I'm never going to see what I become.

Everything fades after that, and when I wake up, the hospital lights are so bright above me that I feel like I might go blind. There's beeping and frantic voices, but it all doesn't feel real.

"You're going to be okay," someone says soothingly to me. But they're wrong. How could I ever be okay again?

"The lights," I croak. Immediately they're dimmed, and I'm able to see more of what's around me. I'm lying in a hospital bed in a generic blue hospital gown. I can see the remnants of my torn shirt on a tray next to the bed with a pair of scissors next to them. Evidently, they had to cut it off. There's a female doctor standing next to the bed. Her brunette hair is up in a ponytail and she's wearing minimal makeup. I don't know why I'm noticing details like that, but I am.

"How did I get here?" I asked, my voice barely recognizable.

She's looking at me with such pity that it makes me want to scream. "One of your neighbors found you passed out in the front yard of your house," she says soothingly as she adjusts an IV that I've just noticed is hooked up to me.

"We need to get a sample for the police, if you're willing," she continues.

"A sample?" I ask confused, until I notice the kit that she's holding in one hand.

"We can also talk about emergency contraceptive measures."

"Emergency contraceptive measures," I murmur as everything suddenly comes into sharp focus.

I begin to thrash wildly in the bed as the images crash down on me. "Help me. Help me," I start screaming.

I'm faintly aware of the doctor barking orders at someone as a pair of hands attempt to hold me down.

But that only makes everything worse.

"Ariana, please calm down. You're safe," someone calls out.

But I'm not safe, because I'm trapped in this never-ending nightmare.

I feel a sharp prick in my arm, and then it all fades away.

When I come to again, all the panic is gone, but in its place is numbness. In its place is a death of my spirit that I don't know how I can ever come back from.

There's a stranger in the room, a kind looking woman with grey streaked black hair. She's sitting in the chair next to my bed, and I've just realized that she's holding one of my hands.

She doesn't speak. She just holds my hand for what seems like hours. I don't think about anything in particular during that time.

I just exist. And maybe that's all I'm capable of doing now.

"Did they swab me?" I finally ask.

She pats the top of my hand. "They haven't yet. They need your permission before they do that."

I nod once, the numbness preventing me from feeling the burning desire for justice that I should be feeling.

"Time is a little bit of the essence right now," she continues. "They need to do the test-" she stops in mid-sentence and clears her throat.

"They need to do the test while it's still fresh," I finish for her, and she squeezes my hand in response.

I turn to look at her. "Will you stay in here with me while they do it?" I ask, somehow needing her to keep holding my hand, even though she's just a stranger to me.

"Of course," she says, and even though I'm pretty sure she must be a counselor for the hospital, and I'm sure she's seen things like this all the time, she still sounds hoarse...like she's going to cry for me.

She presses the button on the bed, and when a voice responds, she tells them that I'm ready.

The next few hours seem hazy, yet I know they will be ingrained in my head for the rest of my life.

They take the sample and then give me two different kinds of emergency birth control.

I'm grateful in that moment more than ever that I ended up in a hospital, because I don't know that I would have been in sound enough mind or in any condition to take anything.

The police are next, and they ask me question after question. I think that having to relive it over and over again is another way that David is able to torture me. At least the first time he violated me, I was high. I'm alert enough now that every detail is like a sharp knife to my soul.

When they leave, the silence in the room is deafening. I'm 18 now, so there's no foster home that I can go to, and there's no way I can go back to that trailer.

My body is bruised, my soul is broken, and I'm homeless and hopeless.

"You'll come to my house," the woman, whose name I've found out is Gene tells me.

Evidently, I had been speaking all of that out loud. Gene is indeed a counselor at the hospital, but I'm convinced that she's secretly an angel in disguise. She hasn't left my side since I woke up. And I'm not sure that I could have gotten through the last few hours without her.

"I can't come to your house," I tell her, tears forming in my eyes.

"Nonsense. You can't take care of yourself, and you certainly can't go back to that place."

"I don't have any money to pay you," I reply hoarsely. She just squeezes my hand and gives me a small, sad smile.

"I would never expect that from you, child."

Gene was a stranger, but she saved my life. I went home with her a few days later.

David overdosed before he could be taken in, so there was no justice for me. Not that a prison sentence could ever have made me whole inside.

I lost pieces of myself that night in my trailer, and I've been searching for them ever since.

14
NOW

ARIANA

I've never heard the kind of quiet that's in this room right now. But it's a heavy kind of quiet. A heaviness bred from sorrow and guilt.

I hate it.

This is why I never wanted to tell them about what happened to me. This is why I pushed them away, why I wanted them to forget that I ever existed. Jesse, Jensen, and Tanner always looked at me like I was something. They didn't see the trailer, the faded clothes, the abuse. They saw me. They needed me. They loved me.

Gene always used to tell me that the shame I felt about what happened to me wasn't right. That I needed to do everything I could to get rid of it.

But I never did.

And now, standing in this room with this silence so thick with pity and shame that I could puke...It's almost more than I can take.

"Say something," I spit out, the words coming out as more of a snarl than anything else.

The glass that Tanner was holding shatters in his hand, spraying the white carpet of the room with a sea of glass and amber liquid.

Jesse sinks into a crouch. He's rocking back and forth, his whole body shaking as great wracking sobs sound out of him.

Jensen's just standing there, staring at me. I can see that his hands are trembling.

"SAY SOMETHING," I scream, and in a mad rage, I rip a picture off the wall and throw it to the ground.

I start crying then, tears that are long overdue. This shouldn't have come as a huge shock to them. I mean, why else do young girls end up scared and alone on exam tables with people taking fucking pictures of them?

I take a vase off a shelf and throw that next, shattering what is most likely a priceless work of art, judging by the rest of the place.

"Baby," Jensen says, and he's there, taking me into his arms, stopping me before I destroy anything else. I beat on his chest. I'm furious at all of them, and I don't know why.

"You're mad because we weren't there, and yet we thought we deserved to know what happened," he says, and his voice is maddeningly calm.

Before Jensen can say anything else, Tanner stalks closer. "Why didn't you fucking say anything to us? Why did you push us away? We could have been there for you." He's crying as he spits his anguish at me.

It only makes me angry, because how dare he ask me those questions, how dare he look at me like this?

I push away from Jensen and walk away, unable to be in the room with them any longer. I stop at the threshold of the door before turning back to look at Tanner. I had one last thing I wanted to say, and then I never wanted to talk about this again.

"After I met you, I would fantasize every night before I went to sleep. We were all in LA. You were big rockstars...I was singing, and people actually wanted to hear it. The images were so clear in my mind that I could see every detail about where we lived, what we sang, how we looked. You know what I fantasized about after that happened?"

Tanner's eyes bored into mine with a deep intensity, but he remained silent.

"Nothing. And that is why I pushed you away. Because the dead didn't belong with the living, and there was nothing alive about me back then.

I'm awake in bed, unable to sleep as I stare at the ceiling. Soft light filters into the room from outside, defining the raised textured pattern around my bedroom's light fixture. I turn my head to see my phone, the numbers 2:36 am shining back at me. I silently pray for sleep to overtake Gentry before he comes in here. I had left him in the living room after he'd beat me again.

It was later than usual, surely that was a good sign.

I tug the comforter up higher over my pajamas, dread anchoring my chest.

Had I even fallen asleep? I wasn't sure.

This is becoming a nightly ritual. Get the shit beat out of me, and then lie in bed for hours, staring at the ceiling, too afraid to allow myself to be pulled into dreams. Sleep was a friend I rarely visited.

The sound of the television clicking off in the living room should have been hard to hear, but I'm as attuned to it as the sound of my own heartbeat, the latter of which starts increasing its boom-boom-boom in dreaded anticipation. My eyes move to the light that frames my closed door in the doorway, and I stare as that light grows dimmer with each flick of a light switch, from the kitchen, to the office, to the hallway. Each click of the light brings the shadows across the floor closer to the bedroom door. Shadows block out light in two spots under the door before I hear the click sound of the light switch just outside. The door to the room is completely shadowed now.

My heart beats twice, fast in my chest. I swear I can hear his breathing just outside my door, and I pray that he will continue walking on to the guest bedroom and somehow decide that tonight was the night he would spare me.

My hopes are dashed a moment later when I hear him humming right against the door. It's the only sound besides the now rapid beat of my heart.

No, no, no, no, I plead uselessly, my fingernails digging into my palms, making fists. The door opens with a creak. The door stops after a few inches, as if he knows I'm awake and is just trying to torture me, even though it's no surprise that he's here. Then the door swings open fully, his face exposed by the light coming through my window.

I sit up in bed, the scream dying in my throat.

In a span of two seconds, a pair of arms are around me, holding me close while telling me that everything will be alright.

It has been a while since I've had a nightmare about Gentry. My brain must have decided to bring them back after the events of the night.

Shakily, I pull myself from the arms that I now recognize as Jensen's, and lift the sheets off my sweat-soaked body and stand up, padding across the floor to my bathroom. I look in the mirror and barely recognize myself. I blow out a tense breath and brush the hair away that clings to my forehead.

The clock on the shelf reads 2:30 AM. Of course.

Taking a deep breath I splash cold water on my face and then go back into the bedroom where Jensen has somehow found his way into my bed, despite the fact that I'm pretty sure that I locked the door before I went to sleep.

Jensen

It's easy for Ariana to get buried in details and overthink until the facts become muddled—lost in her mind and the past. She's survived too much, and now an added tragedy I want to erase. If I went to her right now where she's standing and begged for her to talk to me she would. If I kissed her she would respond. I could strip her bare and murmur my apologies into her ravaged skin, and she would let me, but this is a hard gamble.

What if I push too hard? Yet if I don't . . .

Maybe my impulse to move her beyond this is because I'm desperate to see forgiveness in her eyes and feel it in the touch of her hand. It's years past us now, but I can't help but feel that I've let her down. I could have tried harder, tracked her down and made her give me answers face to face before letting her go. Instead, I took her deadbeat mother's word like a coward and left her alone. Ariana would never have been able to hide from me what happened back then.

She's strong. Stronger than I ever imagined. And her standing there in front of us tonight, a defiant tilt to her chin, just solidified it for me. There's no one like Ariana Kent.

My life is a series of before and afters: before my mother's death and after my mother's death. Before I discovered music and after I discovered music. Before I moved to LA and after I moved to LA.

But the before and after that was the most vivid in my mind was before I met Ariana, and after I met Ariana. And I needed her to know that, even if she didn't know anything else right now.

"I love you," I whisper suddenly, desperate for her to know the truth of that statement in her heart.

"I know," she responds, taking a step closer, and then another step, and then another.

When she finally gets close enough for me to touch her, the only thing I can do is to kiss her. Kiss away history and the uncertainty surrounding the present. Her tongue sweeps into my mouth with the same urgency, until it's not enough, and I want more. More Ariana. Forever and ever.

I just hope that my kiss says everything that my words cannot. I'm sorry. I'm here for you. You'll never be alone again.

I hope she feels the promise in my kiss. Because it's a promise that I won't ever break again.

Ariana

I wake up an hour after I've finally fallen asleep. And this time, it's not because I had a nightmare, this time it's because I need him. I can feel the heat of his chest at my back, and my pulse races. His breathing is shallow, and I'm sure he's just as awake as I am right now.

That's confirmed when I'm suddenly flipped around, and I'm in his arms. My gasp is muffled by his lips, and I want him with an instant urgency. My hands are nestled in his hair, and I cling to him, feet barely skimming the floor. Jensen's touch is tempting, seductive as he removes everything between us—nothing separates him from me, and we come together, skin against skin.

Enfolding me in his arms, he worships my mouth with his; my body heats under his touch as he caresses every whispered shadow. He captures my groan, taking it in to mix with his. I whimper as he kisses across my cheek to my ear and down my neck, nibbling at the hollow above my collarbone. My hands move; they're everywhere, his shoulders, arms, running over the hard lines of his back. Everything he does taunts the wicked pulse between my thighs. Without warning, he pushes me from my side to my back, but he doesn't follow. His breath falters as he gazes. Slow and deliberate, his inspection is thorough, and his voice rough. "I want you. I'll always want you."

I can't help but stare at the glorious specimen in front of me. "Seeing you like this, it doesn't seem real. I used to dream about what it would be like to be with you this way. What it would be like for you to want me as much as I want you. It's almost too much," he whispers, and his eyes change. The passionate need is replaced with veneration, a worshiping glint as he drinks me in. "Ariana," he breathes into the silence, my name a prayer on his lips. Slowly, he lies with me, bringing a hand up to cup the full weight of my breast. Closing his eyes, he leans in so his mouth hovers over mine, not touching, just taking. It's so intimate, but I want to kiss him.

"Jensen," I whisper, and the word breaks the spell. When his eyes open, a devilish gleam replaces the adoration. He pinches the tip of my breast, pulling it until I moan. The sweet sensation drives straight down to my groin, a sharp, inescapable fluttering. He smiles, a slow, beguiling grin as I writhe beneath his dark stare and the attention of his fingers.

"I'm going to taste you, baby. Lick and bite you until you scream my name."

My mouth forms a perfect O, but I say nothing, paralyzed with anticipation. I watch as he dips down, taking me into his mouth, worshipping my skin with his tongue before teasing it between his teeth. I lean back into the bed, reeling from the pleasure his mouth brings. He plays with me until I'm wet and hungry for him.

"Please," I beg for I don't know what. For him to continue, for him to touch me, for him to bring an end to the burning need building between my thighs. Slowly, he moves, his nose trailing along my skin, teasing a path that threatens to drive me crazy. Eyes trained on mine, he pushes my thighs apart.

"You're intoxicating." His voice is hot, his breath hotter as he blows against me.

Looking up through his lashes, he asks, "Do you want this, baby? Tell me you need this as much as I do."

I'm speechless, so he blows against me again.

"Say it; I need to hear you."

"Yes," I barely breathe out before his head dips, the tip of his tongue swirling around me in that perfect spot. My body arches off the bed at the sweet carnal sensation, and I moan loudly.

Closing my eyes, I focus on him, and the tormenting flicks of his tongue. Wrapping his arms under my hips, he becomes impassioned, groaning as he lifts me to his mouth. I can't move, my only outlet the incoherent words falling almost soundlessly into the still air. Clenching my hands into the sheets, I surrender to the beautiful intensity, panting.

"Jensen," I cry. His lips close around me even more. I arch and instinctively move with him, a wicked, slow dance. The music is his mouth, playing artfully, and all I can do is wait, longing for the crescendo. Releasing my death grip on the sheets, I grab the soft silk of his hair. He looks up, eyes scorching and perfect, his tongue insistent and hot, teasing but not taking me over the edge.

"Please," I whisper, begging for the push from the burning plateau. His answer is to slide a finger inside my welcoming body. I groan again. The longing and desire build, the friction of his finger along with his mouth take me higher, faster than I thought possible. I writhe against him, the dance becoming feverish. I need; I want. "Don't stop."

Two fingers plunge into me once, twice, his tongue flicks and rolls again and again, and he launches me beyond the brink. I explode, screaming out in awe as the crescendo hits violently. Waves of pleasure crash through my entire body, and I bow into him once more. His mouth and fingers continue moving on me, in me, pushing my orgasm on and on. When I can stand it no more, I tug his hair, pulling him up to me. Diving into his mouth, I taste myself on his tongue, relishing the feel of his lips stroking over mine. Without thought, I grab his bottom lip between my teeth, sucking on it, mimicking what he just did to me. Drinking in his low moan, I spur him on for more.

"What do you want, baby?"

"I want you."

"What do you need?" he taunts me again.

"You, always you—now," I say, pulling him to me.

In one swift move he enters me, and I cry out as my body acclimates to the invasion. Before I can form a coherent thought, Jensen rolls so I'm on top, straddling his hips. He's now reaching inside of me in a new way, a full tormenting stretch. We groan together when I rotate my hips, deepening the feeling. Our eyes lock, the intensity staggering. Leaning down, I place my hands on either side of his face, cradling him tenderly. My mouth hovers over his, not touching, just taking. Taking him into me every way I know how. His breath, his body, we become one, and I begin to make love with Jensen Reid—sweet, beautiful, passionate love. I feel it all. I feel all of him. My hips move, rounding gently at first, pulling him in and out at a taunting, tortuous pace. Our breaths mingle together, held tight against us as our bodies join, again and again, over and over. In time, I push up, sitting on him fully so he sinks in farther, a new humbling depth that has us both groaning again in unison. Our rhythm changes, needing, wanting, an inexplicable desire to come together as we move passionately. The joy in this moment, in us, is achingly sweet.

"Jensen," I whisper as our eyes meet, his a burning green, mine bewildered by the staggering emotion I feel toward this man. This man who has always been there for me, no matter what he thinks. My thoughts scatter, frayed with unbridled tension, and I dissolve around him, mind and body surrendering to the mystifying connection. I cry out as his hips push me higher, rocketing with him, trusting in wherever he takes me, and I come. I erupt around him, vaguely hearing his cry as he joins me. We are one; we are us. My breath shattered, I fall, splayed out on his chest. His hands wrap into my hair, holding me tight as our bodies calm. Eventually, he pulls my lips to his, kissing me gently. We breathe into each other, sated.

I won't let my past take this away from me.

I can't survive without it.

15
THEN

ARIANA

We're at the beach house again. The guys are surfing, and I'm sitting by the fire they made, laughing and cheering them on. Ever since that first day they brought me here, it's become one of my favorite places. Just sitting here, doing nothing in particular, eating snacks and lazing around...it can't really be beat. Today though, my mind isn't as carefree. Today I'm thinking about the scars all over Tanner's back.

"Ariana?" I'm startled out of my thoughts by Tanner's voice. I shake my head, clearing away my thoughts.

"Hey." I take a drink of my Diet Coke and look up, losing my breath for a second at the image of Tanner, wet, his golden skin glistening in the sun.

"You looked pretty serious over here, you missed Jensen's epic crash," he tells me with a smirk, settling down in the seat across from me and watching me with those silver eyes.

I shrink under his gaze, sure he can see all the way inside of me right now.

He finally looks away, looking back towards the sea where

Jensen and Jesse are still surfing. We sit there quietly for at least half an hour.

"Tell me something no one else knows about you," he asks suddenly, turning his eyes back to me.

I look at everything but him as I try to think of what to say.

The silence stretches awkwardly between us, and before I finally speak, he interrupts. "We don't have to play this game. It was stupid to ask in the first place."

This is my out. I want to take it, but I feel guilty. I've seen pieces of him that I'm pretty sure no one else has. And besides, it's just a game. Why am I even acting like this?

"I can't imagine being happier than this." A truth.

"I don't believe that," he replies. I can't help the bubble of laughter. He doesn't believe this one thing, because I haven't been truthful about anything else about my life. He looks at me quizzically at my outburst. "There isn't anything out there in the whole world that you think would make you happier?"

"Tell *me* something that no one else knows about you," I respond, avoiding the question because how do you tell a boy you've only known for a short blip in time that you think you'll love him and his friends forever? Or that they've given you the only happiness you've ever really experienced, so you can't even comprehend anything better?

I watch Tanner chew on his lip, deep in thought. He leans back into the camp chair and rubs a hand over his chin. "You're right, this is a stupid game," he says with a smirk before popping the top off a beer he picks up from the cooler next to him. He takes a long sip of his beer before getting up and heading to the shed that houses most of the beach equipment. Before I can ask what he's doing, he returns with a guitar case. My heart thuds in my chest for some reason, even though I've seen them all play a million times at this point.

"Do you mind?" he asks as he pulls the guitar out of its case. I shake my head and watch, enraptured, as he starts tuning the guitar. A moment later, he's playing it. The intro sounds familiar, but I can't place it. And then he starts singing. I'll never get tired of his voice. Soft, yet full-bodied. Deep, gravely, and smoky. It's tangled sheets, and stolen kisses. It's perfection.

It takes me a minute, but then I recognize the song. It's "Outnumbered" by Dermot Kennedy. This song has always made me ache. You can hear the longing in the words, the self-loathing, the wish for a different life. This song is Tanner.

I listen closely to the lyrics while he strums along on the guitar. I shiver, feeling transparent. Thankfully, he isn't looking directly at me while singing, so he doesn't see the nerves that flood me, making me want to itch my skin.

When he finishes, his eyes meet mine. He smiles sheepishly. "I love that song. It's my favorite of theirs."

Not wanting to dissect the lyrics, I try diverting the subject. "How long have you been playing?" Jensen told me his story, but I hadn't heard Jesse or Tanner's yet.

Tanner's hands roam over the neck of the guitar, a movement that makes me antsy for some reason. "About five years." I'm sure my eyes betray how surprised I am at that, thinking he had been playing for longer, because he laughs. "If you can believe it, I was kind of a shy kid in elementary and the beginning of middle school."

I smile, enthralled at the unfamiliar light in his eyes as he talks.

"There was a girl I had a crush on, Jennifer, I think was her name. She moved freshman year of high school. But I wanted her to pay attention to me so bad. I tried out for football in 8th grade for her. Hated every second of it, by the way, but I thought she would notice me if I played. Turns out she was more into music than sports. So I joined a guitar class next semester with grand ideas of wooing her with music."

I laugh, unable to think of Tanner having to work to woo anyone. He always held a certain something about him that drew eyes in every room. "So? Did it work out for you? Did you woo her?"

Tanner laughs with me. "No. She saw right through me and was not impressed, to say the least."

"What?" I was surprised. "What girl wouldn't be impressed that you went out of your way to play a song for her?"

"Well, that was part of the problem, actually," he said. He set the guitar with its back on his legs. "She thought I was stalking her and told everyone I was obsessed with her. Kind of embarrassing, actually. That kind of ended my crush."

"Maybe she was on to something. You do always manage to find me. Perhaps you and Jensen and Jesse are all secret stalkers."

"Nah, I think it's just that you want to be found." His eyes meet mine, and though he's teasing, it feels like there's a double meaning to his words. I try to play it off with a smile. I point to the guitar.

"Are you taking requests?" I ask, flirting badly.

Tanner puffs out his chest in complete exaggeration. "Sure am."

"Hmm…" I narrow my eyes in contemplation and tap a finger to my forehead. "How about some Beach Boys?" I ask, snickering since I know for a fact that Tanner doesn't listen to them.

Tanner's lips spread into a boyish grin as he launches into "God Only Knows." I mouth along the words with him, adding as much drama as possible. It's more fun than I've had with him before, and Tanner doesn't pause before he moves from song to song.

He plays a few songs I don't know, so I just lean back and bask in his voice, in the sky darkening as the sun slides down the sky. He sings "Cannonball" by Damien Rice for his last song, and his voice takes on a different quality. His voice takes on an even more gravelly sound, whether by design or from overextending his vocals, I'm not sure. But as with everything he does, I'm mesmerized.

When he sings "It's not hard to fall..." I feel goose bumps prickle my arms, and something squeezes in my chest. After he finishes "Cannonball," the other guys arrive, and the moment is broken.

Jesse and Jensen are starving after surfing for hours, so we cook chicken kabobs over the fire, and the guys laugh and joke and give each other a hard time as I listen and smile, basking in all that is them.

After dinner, it's time to leave. And like always, I wish we didn't have to go and return to the real world.

Tanner drove today, and he arranges it so that he's dropping off Jensen and Jesse before me. The guys give us knowing glances, but the jealousy that I keep expecting never rears its head.

We drive to the drop-off spot, and Tanner gets out and opens my door for me.

It takes only a second before his arms are sliding around my waist, pressing my chest to his. He kisses me like I'm the air he needs to breathe. The anxiety in my veins about going home for the night is overpowered by the instantaneous lust that ripples through every part of my body. I always think that by kissing them, I'll eventually calm the ache I feel whenever I'm around them.

Instead, I always feel like I'm drowning in them, desperate for buoyancy in the sea of my need.

I let my hands tangle in his hair, dragging my nails across his scalp. Tanner's hands move to the back of my head as he pushes me back against the car with little force. One hand moves into my hair, and he twists his fingers into my long locks, tugging on them just enough to tilt my head back. His lips leave mine to travel along my jawline, slowly, kissing just behind my earlobe, before making their way back to my mouth, brushing his facial hair against my skin along the way.

All the breath rushes out of my lungs, and I gasp for air as his lips crush against mine over and over again. One of my hands moves down to cup his jawline. He nips at my upper lip and then my lower lip before sucking my bottom lip into his mouth. My knees grow weak, and I grip the back of his neck with more force than before. Something warm and heavy settles deep in my chest, depriving my lungs of the little remaining breathing room. Tanner pulls away and rests his cheek against mine, each of us trying to catch our breath. We're still tightly pressed together, his heartbeat rapidly echoing off of mine. My chest heaves as I gulp air and try to calm the storm raging within me. His arms slide over my shoulders, hands bracing against the car. His upper arms rest gently on top of my shoulders in this position, sort of like a loose hug, and I run my hands down his biceps, holding him in place, steadying myself. His weight on me is comforting, and I soak in the feeling. I'm completely oblivious to our surroundings, and suddenly thankful this road is not a busy one at this time of night. I feel Tanner's warm breath tickle my ear as our breathing levels out.

"Thanks," I whisper right into his ear.

I feel his returning smile against my cheek before he puts his mouth right by my ear. "You asked me to tell you something no one else knows, but I'd never want to hide this secret."

My breath hitches as his words float over me.

"Ari, I'm in love with you, and I can't imagine being happier than this," he whispers. And then he moves, and I'm walking back to my trailer, only faintly aware of him driving away.

I'm floating on air for the rest of the night, because I love him too.

16
NOW

ARIANA

Clark rings me early the next morning while I'm still tangled up with Jensen.

"Go on Spotify," he demands without a hello. I feel like my stomach is making its way out of my mouth as I switch over to the music app.

"Okay," I tell him, not seeing anything with my name on it. I get up slowly off the bed and go into the hallway so that I don't wake up Jensen.

"Go to the new music Friday playlist," he tells me.

It's a playlist that I watch avidly so I can be sure to know when all my favorite artists release. There was a while there that I felt like I was stalking it as I was desperate to hear the guys' music as soon as it released.

I click the playlist. And there, sitting at number three on the list, is my song.

Clark must've heard my soft gasp because he gives a loud whoop that is very unlike him. "I guarantee that will be number one in the next hour," he says proudly.

I eye the list doubtfully as a very famous female artist has just released a single off of her highly anticipated album today as well.

"We've got to get going," he says. "The label's got a jet for you booked to leave at 1 PM. I'll need you on it and headed to New York for the next week. I'll have the guys join you in two days since we need Tanner to perform that song with you live a few times, and I'm sure Jensen and Jesse will want to talk about what the songwriting process is with you."

"New York City?" I ask, still a little stunned that my name is on a song on Spotify.

"Yes. Now get moving. You'll be back next week to finish the rest of the album."

I'm not speaking, and I know he was expecting more of reaction.

"Ariana, you told me this is what you wanted," he reminds me, his voice disappointed at the thought that I changed my mind. Not that I really could change my mind, the wheels were already turning.

"I'm just in shock. I'm ready for this, more ready then you can believe." I push aside the fact that I'm still having nightmares and panic attacks. The panic attacks had actually gotten a lot better, but after last night... No, I can't think like that. Gentry doesn't get a place in this.

"Something happened last night, Clark. I think Gentry is nearby. He dropped off some documents with the guys, medical records that he shouldn't have been able to get a hold of." I tell him, knowing that my security will need to be apprised of all of that while I'm in New York.

"Fuck. Wait...medical records. Are you pregnant?" he asks hesitantly.

"No," I quickly tell him. "The records are old." And then I open my mouth and say something I never thought I would say out loud, and that now I've said repeatedly over the last 24 hours. It feels like I have to though, because I'm sure Gentry is going to find a way to use the information against me to hurt my career. "Clark, I was raped in high school by my stepfather. It's why I was separated from the guys to begin with," I tell him, the words coming out rough and jagged.

There's a hiss from Clark, and then several muttered expletives. "I'll handle it," he says curtly. "And I'll see you later this afternoon."

I admitted my darkest secret to an almost stranger, and I didn't die or break out in tears. Maybe last night's emotional disaster was what I needed to push me past it.

"I've got to go," he says. "Get packed...and Ari, I'm so damn proud of you," he tells me before hanging up.

I stare at the phone for a minute, and then click over to my song and listen to it. I'd obviously listened to it a million times while recording it, but there's something about listening to it from my phone, from a music streaming service, that's making it sound even better.

Jesse walks into the room just then. His features are drawn, but when he sees me smiling so widely, a smile springs up on his face as well.

"What's going on, pretty girl? Not that I'm complaining about your beautiful smile."

I don't answer him, I simply play the song for him, watching as his smile becomes almost supersonic. He practically flies over to me, and looks at the phone, seeing that it's playing on Spotify.

"Guess Clark wanted to surprise you. This is the best," he tells me, suddenly picking me up and spinning me around while laughing delightedly. Tanner and Jensen both appear, I'm sure because of the ruckus that Jesse's making.

There are laughs and shouts echoing through the hallway. And I just can't believe that after last night, after the terrible words that were spoken, we can be here not even 24 hours later, celebrating.

Suddenly I see the time at the top of my phone. "Shoot, I need to start packing."

"Packing?" Jesse asks, a frown reappearing on his face.

"Evidently, I have some media appearances in New York City," I respond, and I know I'm smiling again at the thought of going back to New York City.

"Well, we're going with you," says Jesse calmly, as he goes to leave the room...I'm assuming to pack.

"It sounds like Clark wanted you guys to come later," I say hesitantly. "I think Clark was going to have Tanner perform with me a few times after I do some interviews by myself," I continue.

"Fuck that, why would we wait a few days when we can be working on finishing your album while we're there?" says Jensen, taking out his phone and beginning to type furiously.

I look over at Tanner to see his reaction, since he's the one that's in our single. But talking to Tanner is evidently still hard. Because he staring off into space as if he's contemplating when he's going to get his next drink, which he probably is thinking about, come to think of it. I thought we had a little bit of a breakthrough the other night, but last night seems to have kicked us ten steps back again.

"Well, we better get all packed then," I tell everyone, garnering surprised stares. I mean yeah, I want this album to be mine, I want to make a name for myself that has to do with my talent, not who I'm dating. But wasn't this our dream to begin with, that we do this all together? And shouldn't I have someone who I know is in my corner, no matter when I'm starting all of this anyway?

Clark can give me all the tips he wants, but he hasn't been the one giving these interviews, the guys have. And this may be my first single, but Tanner's the other voice on it, and I wrote the song with Jensen. It seems selfish of me to try and take all of the credit now.

Ignoring their confused stares at the fact that I'm being so reasonable, I go back into my room and begin to open drawers and pull out clothes, opening my email every now and again to look at some of the suggestions that the band stylist has given me in the past for outfits. I'm sure that Clark will have clothes that he wants me to wear, but I want to feel like myself when I'm doing all of this, since I'll be out of my comfort zone to begin with.

The guys haven't moved, and I clap my hands together. "Come on, if you're going with me, we've got to be on that plane at 1 o'clock," I order. And that seems to finally break them out of whatever trance they're in and get them moving. Jesse and Jensen disappear first, but Tanner hovers near the doorway.

I look at him expectantly.

"Just for the record, Princess," he begins. "You're the best singing partner I've ever had," he continues, before he disappears out of the room.

Tanner makes my heart hurt. He's so frustrating, but at the same time, I can feel his love for me. All I can pray is that he's able to push through his demons and get us back to where we were. The guilt that he's creating in his head isn't real. If I don't blame him for Miranda's actions, or for giving up on me all those years ago, he shouldn't blame himself either.

Shaking off my thoughts, I finish packing and head downstairs where the car Clark sent is waiting. The driver doesn't seem surprised when we all pile outside, and I guess Jensen informed Clark of the change in plans.

The privacy wall between the driver and our seats is open, and I can hear the radio playing a top hits station. Just then, a familiar song starts to play and I literally scream...making all the guys jump. Luckily, the driver is still putting the bags in the back and not driving yet, so I don't make him crash.

It's my song. It's actually playing on the radio. I know I've just seen it on Spotify, and that technically streaming is where everything is nowadays, but there's still something about hearing your song play on the freaking radio. It just makes it real.

Jesse pulls out a bottle of champagne that's been chilling in the cooler, and pops it open, pouring the bubbly liquid into a plastic cup. "To our lady, the most talented, beautiful woman in the world," he says handing it to me with a flourish.

I blush, feeling a little tipsy already off the adrenaline that's flowing through my veins, despite the fact that I haven't taken a sip of alcohol yet.

Jesse finishes pouring everyone else cups, and we toast again, all the guys giving me their sexiest smiles, tempting me with thoughts of how nice it would be to be alone with them.

I manage to restrain myself from jumping them, and thirty minutes later, we're at the private airfield where the label's plane is waiting. Tanner jokes about how they're giving me the red carpet treatment, and that they didn't get to use the private plane when they were first starting, but I'm only halfway listening because I still can't get over the fact that I'm about to fly on a plane that's been sent for me especially. My phone buzzes just then, signaling a text is coming in. Reading it, my jaw drops. It's Clark informing me that the song is currently sitting at number two on the Billboard charts.

"That's my girl," Jesse whispers, brushing a kiss against my cheek as he reads the text over my shoulder. We're led to our seats by an attractive male employee, and I don't miss how the guys intentionally bracket me on all sides, and how Jensen keeps his hand on my knee, shifting closer to me every time Donovan, the steward, comes by to check on us.

Despite my excitement, I fall asleep on the flight, extremely tired since I only got a few restless hours of sleep last night. Jesse gently wakes me up as we're beginning our descent. Seeing the New York skyline spread out before me like a plate of opportunity causes me to choke up. LA may have been the place where I always dreamed about making it big, but there's something about New York City.

As soon as we land, we're shuttled into waiting cars where an annoyed looking Clark is waiting for us.

"Good to see you, darling," says Clark, brushing a light kiss on my cheek. The last month has seen Clark and I developing what I think is an actual friendship. And I've grown more and more comfortable with the idea that he has my best wishes in mind.

"Boys," he drawls, mock annoyance in his voice. Something tells me that Clark knew it wasn't going to go over well coming alone today. "Everything okay then, Ari?" Clark asks, and I know that he's talking about what I told him earlier.

I give him what I hope looks like a genuine smile, because I am hopeful that everything will be okay. I face timed with Dr. Mayfield this morning before we got on the plane, and she gave me a couple of thought exercises to help calm me down if I started to experience a panic attack on the trip. She'd been proud of me for finally telling the guys.

I was proud of myself too. I felt lighter today, almost like I could do anything.

I don't have time for much introspection though, because Clark hands me a piece of paper and I see that I probably won't be sleeping for the next week, as he's packed my schedule with interviews with what seems like a million people. And it starts right now.

Clark proceeds to give me a lecture about what questions to expect and how I should answer them. "I've specifically told them not to ask any questions about your relationship with the guys," he tells me, and I nod.

Tanner curses. "Are you trying to push us out of Ari's life, or are you just an asshole?" he spits at Clark, who looks taken a back.

"I've talked about this with Ari and we've agreed that we

want the focus to be on her music, not on her relationships with the three of you.

I look at Jensen and Jesse and they also look hurt by the idea.

"If we allow those questions, that's all they'll ask about. What we created will get lost," I try and explain.

"Pretty girl, our music is us," Jesse says gently. "We've made that very clear in all our interviews since you came back into our lives."

"How about this...we won't tell them they're allowed to ask the questions, but I won't refuse to answer them if they do ask," I say, looking at all three of them.

Jesse and Jensen nod reluctantly, but Tanner still looks pissed. But I choose to ignore him. It doesn't feel like anything can get Tanner in a good mood lately.

We get to the first interview just then, it's one of the biggest radio stations in the country. After this, we'll have dinner with some label executives and then we will have to get to bed early for an early morning interview on The Morning Show.

I'm fiddling with my clothes as we walk into the building. The radio hosts look surprised and then delighted to see the guys with me. They start to ask them questions, but Clark immediately holds up his hand.

"The guys won't be answering questions. They're just here for moral support, since they contributed to the song. Please continue with your questions for Ariana."

The radio host, DJ Tom, looks annoyed but quickly recovers and begins to pepper me about the song, my writing process with Jensen, and what Tanner is like to sing with.

The interview is going well I think until we get to the end.

"So, Ariana," DJ Tom begins, a sneaky smile on his face as he begins his last question. "Rumors are going crazy that you're actually dating the whole band...what do you have to say about that?"

Clark looks like he's going to throttle him, but I'm more worried about what the guys think. I know Clark would want me to deny it for now, but looking at them, I can't bring myself to do it. The Sound of Us have owned my heart since the moment they came into it. I don't think that I could ever deny that, not after everything we've been through to get to this point.

I take a deep breath. "Our relationship is private, and we would like to keep it that way. But I can tell you that I have loved these boys since I was a teenager, and that's never going to change."

Clark ends the interview and hustles us out without letting me say goodbye and with a well-placed glare at DJ Tom. We get into the back of the car, and Jensen is on me. He grinds into me, and as soon as I open my mouth to respond, his lips take mine in a desperate kiss. When his tongue sweeps into my mouth, I moan and grip his hair, pulling myself flush against the lines of his chest. His hands knead, touch, and roam over every inch of my back while his mouth continues its devastation. He tastes good, like champagne and something new, something that's been out of my reach until now. I vaguely hear Clark calling our names, but I don't care. I grip Jensen harder, kissing him longer. This is what I want forever and ever with all of them.

Jesse finally pulls Jensen away with a big grin on his face. "Fuck, I love you," says Jensen, obviously happy with my answer to that last question. Looking at the other two, they're practically beaming as well. Even Tanner is cracking an uncharacteristic grin.

"So, I guess I did good?" I joke, and Clark moans as Jesse tries to jump me for a kiss.

"We don't have time for this," he says, pulling Jesse away and forcing me to sit in the front seat. "We're on a schedule and due for that dinner in ten minutes, and we're twenty minutes away."

We make it to the dinner, and it's ridiculously boring. I just want to sing, I'm realizing that the rest of the politics involved with that are the baggage that come with that. Everything changes when a server comes in with a giant cake. It's at least three feet tall and covered in gold sprinkles. There's a giant number one on the top of the cake with tall sparkler looking candles all over it.

I look at the guys confused, but they've got big grins on their face. The VP of the label stands up just then. "A toast to 'The Last Night of You' becoming Billboard's newest #1 song," he croons, and the whole room erupts in applause. I have to sit down at the news, because I feel like I'm having a heart attack. It's only when Jesse pulls it up on his phone to show me that I can really believe it.

I spend the next hour accepting congratulations with people I don't even know...but I'm not bored anymore.

This is one of the greatest days of my life.

The next few days are the busiest of my life. Every single second of my time has been planned, but we still haven't gotten to perform the song live yet. So when we get to the Spotify studio for Tanner and I's first live performance, I'm ready.

I slip into the dressing room that Tanner has been hanging out in since we got here.

"You ready?" I ask, hating how awkward I feel with him right now. I keep thinking that it will get better, but it never does. And even though Tanner looks his gorgeous bad boy self this afternoon, I know for a fact that he was woken up by Clark an hour ago because he'd gotten black out drunk last night after dinner.

"I'm always ready," he smirks, but it comes out half-hearted.

I open my mouth to say more, desperate to pull him towards me and shake some sense into him, but our Spotify handler for the day chooses that moment to knock on the door, signaling that it's time for us to start.

My nerves are next level for this, and I'm worried I'm going to mess up like I did for most of my first takes in the recording studio thus far.

But as soon as the music starts, I lose myself in the ebb and flow of the notes, and the rhythm of my heart changes to match the music—slow and easy. Tanner's voice glides in with the gravelly, honest sound that has won the hearts of millions around the world. When I chime in with the harmony, our voices blend beautifully, rising and falling in crescendo. Our eyes lock, and the passion of the music plays out in our faces. Around the room, everyone is avidly fixed on us as we perform. I've never felt so alive yet so completely vulnerable, and even Tanner, with all his angst, can't help but feel this moment with me. He's smiling while he sings with me, his eyes never straying away from me as he sings his verse.

When we sing the last line, "The last night of you, meant the last night of me," Tanner tips his head so that our foreheads are touching and our lips are a whisper apart. The room is silent for a moment, and then it erupts in a fury of applause, catcalls, and whistles.

Tanner gives me a soft kiss before he begins to withdraw himself. And by the time the applause dies down, the smile is gone, and he's just as cold and untouchable as before we started. I frown at him but try to concentrate on the people that have come over to talk to us. I would have almost preferred that he stayed withdrawn instead of offering me a glimpse of the boy that I'm desperately hoping to get back.

It's going to be a long rest of the week.

17

THEN

ARIANA

There was another party at Tanner's house. There haven't been any while his parents were in town. But the second they left the country to go back to London, Tanner sent out an open invite for people to come over.

His parents had been here for two months while his father tended to business, which didn't seem that long in retrospect, but the damage they had done to Tanner in that time was tangible.

It took me a little while to come over. David and my mother had been having a full on brawl when I came home from school today. The police were called, and I had to try to cover for them so that I didn't get taken to a foster family and end up who knows where. Despite how bad everything was, I heard the stories about the nightmares kids found themselves in in some foster homes, and I felt much more comfortable facing the evil I did know rather than the evil I didn't.

For some reason, I don't tell the guys why I'm late, I don't tell them about my stepdad walking in on me while I was getting dressed, the way his eyes danced across my body as I tried to hide it from view. I don't tell them about how I threw up afterwards because I felt so sick about the look that was in his eyes.

I don't tell them that I walked to Amberlie's house, and then I cried when I got there.

I don't tell them about any of that.

Maybe it's because they have so many of their own problems, between Tanner and Jensen. And Jesse, who's always trying to keep them together...I don't want to add more to their burdens.

I've never had someone look at me the way that they do, and the thought of risking that by telling them what my life is really like...I just couldn't handle it if they ever did look at me like they felt sorry for me. I've had enough pity from people in my life to last nine life times.

Apparently, my extreme tardiness accounts for the reason why Tanner is so drunk he can't see straight when I arrive. At least he seems to recognize me, pulling me into a full body hug that threatens to send me to the ground, since he's having trouble standing himself.

Jesse has evidently gotten tired of watching out for Tanner because he's drunk as well.

After the drunken fight that I just witnessed at home, the last place I really want to be is around a bunch of drunk people.

I leave Amberlie with some of her cheerleader friends and I walk out to the back deck where I find Jensen smoking a blunt with a couple of their crowd from school, the smoky tendrils fading into the night air. I sneeze from the skunky smell, bringing Jensen's attention to me. He jumps in surprise to see me, and then looks a little bit guilty for me catching him smoking. He hands it to his friend and stands up to greet me.

"Hey, baby," he says to me. He doesn't kiss me just then, in front of his friends, but I can see that he wants to. And I wonder why he stops himself. "You're late," he says instead of kissing me.

I look at him with an eyebrow raised. "Did you actually notice?" I ask, gesturing to his group of very high friends. He winces.

"I'm always thinking about you and wanting you with me," he replies, and it catches me off guard because there's so much earnestness in his voice. I smile shyly at him. He opens his mouth to say something just then, but is cut off when Tanner stumbles outside.

"Princess," he yells out. And I can feel the eyes of everyone who's out here on me. "Princess," he yells again, obviously not seeing me because of Jensen standing in the way.

"Tanner?" I ask softly, hoping that will get him to be a little bit quieter. All the attention is making me want to break out in hives.

"There you are," he says, holding up his drink like he's cheering me. He stumbles over to me, stopping himself so awkwardly that he sloshes his drink all down the front of my shirt.

I let out a little cry because his drink is cold against my skin, and this was one of Amberlie's white blouses that I borrowed for the party. And now it's ruined, thanks to the red punch he was drinking that smells like it's mostly vodka with a lot of red food coloring.

"What the fuck is wrong with you, man?" Jensen growls at Tanner before pushing him away from me.

I kind of feel like crying after what happened at my house, and now this.

And I'm suddenly extremely tired.

"Jensen, it's fine," I tell him in a resigned voice. But he cuts me off.

"No Ari, it's not fine. This tool has been walking around with his head up his ass for a month now, and he won't tell us why. Having crappy parents doesn't give you an excuse to act like a dip shit," he spits at Tanner. A crowd's been building around us, and they all go quiet.

"What did you just say to me?" Tanner slurs. "Why don't you tell yourself that, since you've been using the loss of your mother to get Ari to spend all her time with you," Tanner snarls at Jensen.

I gasp, not believing that those words just came out of Tanner's mouth.

"Okay guys, let's just take a break before anything else is said," I plead with them. But they're not backing down from each other. I look around for Jesse, hoping that he'll step in. But he's still inside. I pull out my phone and send a quick text, hoping that Jesse's not too drunk to read it.

This is why I stayed away from parties my whole life. Nothing good ever comes from them.

"We both know you'll do anything to get her attention. Why don't you ask her who she kissed the other night? Ask her if she liked it, if it made her wet. Ask her who she thinks about when she's in her bed touching herself," Tanner says wickedly.

And now I'm not just sick about the situation, I'm furious. How dare he talk about me like that in front of all these people, in that tone, like our kiss meant nothing and I'm just a sex toy to be passed around the three of them. We're not even having sex...but I guarantee everyone out here is going to think that.

"Jesse has the nice guy golden boy routine going on, and you know he's in there good with her. What do you have to offer her, Jensen?" Tanner keeps talking, his vile words springing from his mouth until I'm not sure that I've ever really known him.

Jesse comes out just then, looking a little green around the gills. "What's going on, guys? Ari just texted me," he says, his words slurring a little as well. He looks around, and sees me standing there, and then sees that half the party is standing outside around the three of us.

Tanner and Jensen are both just staring at each other. Their looks are full of loathing. They're the kind of looks that I've only ever seen them reserve for other people, never for each other.

Just then Tanner and Jensen also look around, and it's as if they thought we were alone this whole time and only just now have noticed everyone else. Tanner's eyes dart towards me, and I know he sees the disgust written all over my face, because a look of shame crosses his features.

"Princess," he begins.

I don't let him talk. "You went too far," I spit at him, actually hating him in this moment. He talked about me like I was trash, like I was just another one of those girls that hung all over them. I was supposed to be his good thing.

Evidently, I was actually nothing.

Drunk or not, there is no excuse for him talking about me like that. I just want to go home, but home would be even worse. I knew after their fights today, I was likely to come home and find Terry and David going at it in the living room.

I feel really alone in this moment.

Tanner takes a step towards me again, and I back away. "Stay away from me, Tanner," I tell him coldly. Tanner clinches his drink tightly, breaking the cup and sending more red punch everywhere. He throws it to the ground. "Fuck," he roars.

He darts back inside, still tripping over himself with how intoxicated he is. A little part of me suddenly feels guilty about talking to him like that, since I know that he's been going through something bad the last month, but I push it away. Everyone has bad shit that happens to them. And we all don't act like assholes.

Jesse walks over to me, and puts his arm around me. "I'm too drunk to drive, and Ubers don't come out here, so let's just go hang in the theater room. Everything will be better in the morning," he tells me, blinking rapidly as he tries to focus on my face. Jensen nods in agreement, looking exhausted all of a sudden, whether from the blunt or from fighting with Tanner. I'm mad at him too for instigating all of that. But we'll talk about it when he's sober.

As we walk into the house, I see that Tanner is playing beer pong with one of his buddies against Reagan and one of her friends. I seethe at seeing him hang out with her, even though he doesn't even seem to be talking to her. He shoots me a wounded look as I pass by him, but I ignore it. Getting more drunk was only going to make everything worse, didn't he know that?

I can't concentrate on the movie, my mind keeps flickering over what happened. Jensen is sulking on the opposite couch while I snuggle into Jesse's arms.

Suddenly the door to the theater room flies open and one of the guys that sometimes joins us at the lunch table, Thomas, comes barreling in.

"Get the fuck out here," he screeches. "Tanner's having a seizure."

We fly out of the room. I let out a sob when I see Tanner on the ground next to the bar, convulsing. He starts to choke on what I assume is his throwup.

I launch myself at him and turn his body to the side. It takes all of my strength, because he's still thrashing around. I don't even think about it when I scoop my fingers into his mouth to help get the throwup out. Jesse is on the phone with 911 while Jensen just stares at us, horrified and a little dazed. I'm only faintly aware of Reagan standing a few feet away from us with her hands over her mouth as she cries. Tanner stops seizing, but the complete stillness of his body is almost worse. His breathing is labored, but at least he's stopped choking.

It seems like it takes an hour for an ambulance to arrive,

just because of how far out Tanner's house is from everything. I wonder what his parents will do when they hear he had to go to the hospital. Will they come back? Would that just make everything worse? I know Jesse did the right thing by calling for help. A blackout with throwing up we could handle, but seizures denoted something totally different.

I had seen enough overdoses with Terry to know that they usually signaled drugs. And even though it was selfish in a time like this, I was a little heartbroken that Tanner had broken his promise to me.

As was my way, I started to blame myself, thinking that I had driven him over the edge by getting mad at him. I push those thoughts away, though, as I often had to do. This was no one's fault but Tanner's.

I was the only one who hadn't been drinking, so I drive the guys as we follow the ambulance. It's a terrifying ride. I have very little experience actually driving even though I've had my license for awhile—just because I've never had a car. Terry and David usually didn't have a car either since every time they got one, they would end up selling it to supply their drug habit.

I feel like I've lived five lives by the time we get to the hospital, and I'm shaking from the adrenaline rush. Driving really isn't that hard, but it started raining during the drive, and I'd barely been able to see the lines in the road.

Tanner is taken immediately inside, but I'd seen him open his eyes as he was wheeled away, and I was hopeful that was a good sign. We sit in the waiting room after that. Well I sit, Jensen is stalking the front desk, barking at the nurse for updates. Jesse is leaning against the wall, his face in one of his hands.

"Do you think his parents will come?" I ask softly.

Jesse looks at me. "I sure as hell hope not," he says bitterly. "If I see them, I don't know what I'll do."

Two hours pass, and people who were at the party file in

and out of the waiting room, which impresses me considering how drunk everyone had been when we left. I realize that we basically left Tanner's mansion filled with drunk high school students. Hopefully, it's still standing.

"Do you think we need to go back to the house and kick everyone out?" I ask.

Jensen shakes his head. "Tanner's family has a house manager. I texted him to kick everyone out and close up shop."

"House manager... hmmm," I say out loud, trying to picture needing one of those. A small smile cracks on Jesse's face. It's the only time that any of us have smiled since arriving.

Just then, a kind looking older man dressed in a white coat comes through the doors into the waiting room. He looks at his clipboard. "Jesse Carroway, Jensen Reid, Ariana Kent?" he calls out, looking around the actually quite crowded waiting room.

I stand up quickly, and Jensen and Jesse stalk over. The doctor looks at Jensen and Jesse a little nervously. Jesse still looks a bit drunk, and Jensen just looks pissed, and a little menacing, if I'm being honest. "I'm Dr. Madison. I've been taking care of Tanner this evening."

"How is he?" I squeak before the doctor can say another word. The doctor smiles gently.

"Mr. Crosby is very lucky. He had a life-threatening amount of cocaine in his blood. Mixed with alcohol, his body couldn't take it. We have him on an IV, and we expect him to make a full recovery, but it would appear to me that Mr. Crosby needs some help." He eyes the three of us. Jesse and Jensen don't exactly look like poster boys of healthy living with their tattoos, piercings, and leather jackets.

"Thank you Doctor. Are we allowed to see him?" I ask.

He nods. "I'll take you to him."

As we walk behind the doctor, I lean over to Jesse and

whisper, "Shouldn't the police have been called if Tanner was found with illegal drugs?" I ask. Jesse rolls his eyes. "I'm sure Leonard made a sizable donation in the family's name to convince them otherwise."

"Leonard?" I ask.

"The house manager," Jesse clarifies.

All of my questions about Tanner's house manager disappear as we walk into the room. Tanner looks like he's sleeping. He's pale with dark shadows under his eyes, but he's still one of the most beautiful things I've ever seen.

I rush over to the bed and take his hand. "You stupid idiot, you could've died," I murmur sadly, thinking he's asleep and can't hear me.

His eyes crack open. "I didn't take any drugs tonight, Ari. You have to believe me," he says in a raspy voice.

I'm conflicted. I was well aware of the fact that addicts lie. Terry had been lying to me for so long that I stopped believing anything that came out of her mouth. But this was Tanner. Even though I was mad at him right now, I still felt like I knew him. I could see the dark ugly parts of him, and they called to me because I had them too. Tanner was a lot of things, but I hadn't ever felt that one of those things was a liar.

"Do you know how they got into your system?" I ask hesitantly. He looks hopeful at the fact that I'm not immediately rejecting what he said. But that hope quickly turns into frustration. "I have no idea. Last I remember, I was playing beer pong... And then I don't really remember anything after that," he says, clenching his jaw.

I know why he just made that face. It was because he remembered that Reagan had been there.

Wait... Just then, I remember her face when Tanner had been seizing up on the floor. It was devastated looking... but it also looked almost guilty.

But that was crazy, right? There's no way that she did something like that.

I can't help but think about how desperate she had been acting lately once Tanner started hanging out with me. She hadn't been able to keep any of her nasty comments to herself...which meant that she had been completely blacklisted from Tanner's life.

Yes, all three of the guys were sexy as hell. And in fact I was attracted to all of them the same, which was weird considering how different they all were. But there was just something about Tanner that called to women. Whether it was the flashing silver eyes, or the sexily mussed up black hair that evoked images of a romp between the sheets, or the face that could make angels weep... Women wanted him. Or maybe it was the brokenness inside of him that called to them.

Whatever it was, every girl we were around wanted to be the one to fix Tanner Crosby.

Little did they know that some people were just unfixable.

"I don't have an explanation, Ari. But I'm asking you to believe me. I fucked things up enough tonight without you thinking that I was snorting lines with a girl I used to hook up with," he says, staring at me pleadingly. He has an iron grip on my hand, and I doubt that I could pull away, even if I wanted to. I realize that he's frightened of what I'm going to do. And it feels strange to realize that he truly cares what I think in this moment and if it means that I will leave him.

I still wasn't used to that, someone actually caring.

Jesse kicks off from where he leaned against the wall. "Why were you even hanging with that bitch in the first place, Tanner?" he asks, the infliction in his voice letting us all know that he thought Tanner had acted like an idiot.

"I wasn't 'hanging' with her," he says petulantly. "She had the table already set up when I came inside and Dorian needed a partner to play. All I wanted to do was get fucked up enough to forget what I had just done," he tells him, shooting me a look again.

"Wait, so Reagan does drugs?" I ask, still unable to get that niggling feeling out of my brain that she was somehow involved in this if Tanner was telling the truth.

Jensen snorts. "Does Reagan do drugs? That's hilarious. How do you think Tanner started hooking up with her in the first place? It wasn't because of her sparkling personality. It was because she always had coke and always had her legs spread."

I flinch at that. We hadn't even come close to sex, and the fact that the guys always stopped before we got too far made me a little bit self-conscious, considering I knew they weren't saints before they met me.

Jesse punches Jensen in the arm, and Jensen looks chagrined. Tonight was just a disaster on all fronts.

"Did they call your parents?" Jesse asks Tanner hesitantly.

Tanner gets stiff at that question. "I'm sure they did, but they're not going to turn their jet around when they just got to 'good old London' to come check up on their son. Not that I'd want them to in the first place," he adds, a haunted look on his face. "I'm sure there will be hell to pay from my dad though," he says, and we all grow quiet after that.

I was pretty sure that his dad was responsible for the injuries I had seen when we had gotten tattoos, and I still wasn't sure what to do about it, or if the other two knew. Somehow it felt like this thing we weren't supposed to talk about.

Tanner looks at me. "I know I don't deserve it, but will you stay?" he asks. And I know he's not just asking if I'll stay at the hospital with him until he gets out. He's asking if I'll stay with him in general.

And I don't know what it says about me that my answer will always be yes.

...

We get out of the hospital the next day. Jesse and Jensen both left to get changed at some point, and I was exhausted, since I only got in a couple of hours of fitful sleep in the armchair next to Tanner's hospital bed. I'm surprised that they're letting him go already, but evidently, with how much hush money his family had given the hospital to prevent Tanner from getting in trouble, Tanner could basically do whatever he wanted as far as medical decisions went.

He was in bad shape, though. The combination of the hangover and coming down from the drugs had him miserable. He sat in Jensen's Escalade, his face in his hands. I was pretty sure that I heard a few moans coming out of him as we drove. Jensen drove us all to Tanner's house. I was surprised to see that Reagan was sitting on the front porch.

When we get out of the car, she flings herself at Tanner, almost knocking him over.

"What the hell, Reagan?" he tells her, pushing her off.

"I was so worried about you," she says, tears building in her eyes. "I didn't mean... I mean it was so bad."

Jensen grabs her arm, surprising me with the vehemence on his face. "Did you have something to do with this?" he asks, giving her a little shake. Jesse's quietly watching, and I can tell he's prepared to step in if Jensen goes too far, not that I think Jensen ever would. He's not the type to beat up girls.

Reagan looks at the three of us, and then seems to realize she can't get out of this because her face scrunches up, and then she tries to lunge at me. When she's not able to get anywhere because of Jensen's grip on her arm, she begins to cry.

It all comes rushing out, how she put drugs in his drink, and they ended up being from a bad supplier. She had just wanted to loosen him up so that he would pay attention to her.

"I love you," she begins screaming at a haunted looking Tanner as Jensen drags her to his car and throws her in the backseat.

Jesse pulls out his phone and calls someone. "We have a situation," he says, and then he hangs up.

A few minutes later a distinguished gentleman comes out of Tanner's house, and Jensen hands him his keys. "Take her home and make sure her parents find the cocaine in her pocket," Jensen tells him.

"Of course," the man says before getting in the car and driving away. I shiver a bit at seeing Reagan staring out the window at us, tears streaming down her face.

"Who was that?" I finally ask, once I get over the shock of what just happened.

"Leonard," Tanner says simply, and the guys all start to walk inside. I stare after them, thinking hard about what I should do.

For the first time since meeting them, I'm not sure that I want to follow them.

18
NOW

JESSE

I hang on her doorframe, watching as she packs. Well, attempts to pack. Now that her album is done, we're all about to go on tour. Except, she will be leaving on her own small tour as an opener for Red Daydreams until she meets back up with us in a few weeks. It will be the first time that we've been apart, and I'm trying not to think about it.

She's also dancing to Drake's "God's Plan" as she's packing right now, making me a little bit horny and delaying said packing.

Not that I mind. Anything that delays her from leaving me sounds like a good idea. Just the thought of her being out of my presence makes my skin itch. I push that thought out of my head. I've had this argument with her a million times, and at this point, I'm just starting to sound unsupportive.

I cross my arms and watch the show as it moves into "7 Rings".

"Nice moves, pretty girl," I murmur when she turns, and her perfect tits bounce through the dance. This is good shit.

Her head snaps up, and she stumbles to the nightstand to switch off her phone.

"Don't stop on my account. That was better than a lap dance."

"You're ridiculous," she mutters, grabbing a pillow from her bed and hugging it to her torso.

My grin grows. "I've seen those pretty breasts before. You think hiding them from me will dissuade my imagination?"

Her gaze narrows in on mine, but then it flicks down to my abs and lowers to the bulge that's growing in my pants. No shower in the world could kill that boner.

She closes her eyes, but her accelerated breath moves the pillow up and down. Good. I like the direction she's headed.

"Jesse?"

"Ari?"

"How long..." She bites her bottom lip, seeming to lose her train of thought as I stalk towards her. "You're so annoying," she finally says lamely.

"Like so annoying, you could tie me up? Because I might like that with you. Or we can role play? I've got this fantasy."

Her mouth falls open, and then she swings the pillow and clocks me on the ear, a sneak attack that takes me off-guard. I don't know if I should be pissed at the assault or thrilled as my predatory nature wakes from sleep. The second hit lands on my hip. I snarl and size up my prey, thinking it's time to steal her weapon. She pants, and the tits I dream about nightly heave, drawing my attention to the way they're straining against the fabric of her shirt.

I stalk toward her. "You sure about this?"

"I've got a good arm, Popeye. You scared?"

I stop and glare at her. "What did you call me?"

She laughs and chucks a pillow at my head. "Popeye the sailor man . . ." she croons.

Oh, fuck no. I advance. She retreats—singing.

She's so fucking hot. Toned muscles, tanned skin, curves

in every damn right place. And it hits me like a ton of feather pillows for the millionth time.

I'm so in love with Ariana Kent.

The desperate ache in my cock is a pressing issue since she's come back into my life, but so is hearing her laugh and seeing her teasing smile every day. I want her voice to fill these walls until they crumble, even when the song is about me eating my spinach. This has moved beyond possession and into a dark cavern I have yet to explore.

By the heavy lurch of my heart, I know that I'm scared of how much I need her. And it scares me that I don't think she needs me in the same way.

The thought unleashes a primal instinct to claim her, take her, make it so no other man but the three of us will ever have her again. But first, I'm going to wipe that grin off her face and make her scream. I pick up a pillow off her bed and advance.

My initial pillow strike misses as she lobs to the left. The second hits her square over the head. Her eyes flare and then narrow, and I can tell the minute tactical thought gives way to a frantic need to conquer her target. She misses a lyric and attacks in reckless swings.

I'm trained in the art of all things Ariana, though, and in a minute, I chase her over the bed and to the other side of the room with quick snaps to the backs of her thighs and a crack to her ass. She twirls with indignation, gripping her backside, and I drop my weapon.

With one arm around her waist, the other on her nape, I haul her against my chest and slam my mouth on hers. Sweet Hell, she kisses me without hesitation, sucking my tongue into her mouth on a groan. We go deep, long open licks I use to punish her for singing that fucking song. It takes every ounce of my self-control not to pin her against the wall, peel off her shorts, and fuck her into an apology.

I'll save that for later.

I tap her ass and help to wrap her legs around my waist, and it's the best, most natural place for her to be. When she wiggles into position, she slides down against my straining dick, and I struggle not to embarrass myself. I moan and tug her hair, peeling her away to find her flushed skin, watching her lowered lids flutter against her cheeks as I rub myself against her through the fine layers of cotton.

"Jesse?" Her voice is as erratic as the pulse pounding in her neck, and full of vulnerability, uncertainty, and dammit, I hate that she's leaving us after how shitty everything has been.

I press my mouth to her forehead and back us up to the plush chair in her room, keeping her legs on either side of my hips as we sit. "It's okay, pretty girl. I've got you. I will always have you."

She pulls back with my face cradled in her hands, her brow pulled in a deep V. "Why are you stopping?"

"I'm not stopping. I'm just slowing us down."

Her chest hitches, but before I can tell if she's crying, she buries her nose in my neck and plasters herself impossibly close to me. I feel everything. Every part of her, the tight peak of her nipples, the soft swell of her swollen breasts, and the fierce grip of her arms around my neck as if the thought of being apart is as disturbing to her as it is to me.

But I just hold her and let our pulses slow into the same pattern while dragging my fingers up and down her spine.

"Jesse?"

"Yes?" I ask, watching her bring her gaze back to mine.

"I'm scared we won't be able to handle this."

Fuck. I don't give her a chance to say anything else. There's no future ahead of me that doesn't have this girl in it, and someday, she's finally going to realize this.

My mouth is on hers, deep and searing, a tangle of tongues and promises I hope I keep. Her lips are firm and hungry, but I'm hungrier, and we fight for control, a wet, hot struggle to destroy the fear that keeps winding its way around us.

I want to make her mine right now, sink my teeth in her flesh, slay the fear that prevents her from finally being all mine.

I fight for it, holding her hips as I grind between her thighs, and we become a writhing, panting mass of need. Reason returns and I break the kiss, pulling away to find her swollen, pink lips parted.

"I want to touch you," she says.

I groan and pin her hands behind her back. She's killing me. "I want that too, but no."

Ari struggles to free herself and growls through her frustration. "Jesse," she whines.

I grab her neck, holding her in a possessive but tender grip as I shift and slide her fingers down my abdomen until they're pressed over my erection. "Do you feel me, pretty girl? That's a fuck ton of inches of pure commitment. Let me know when you finally accept this is forever, and I'm not ever going anywhere."

She smiles. A lazy grin peels across her face, and she squeezes me.

"Ari," I warn through clenched teeth.

"Shh. Let me have what I want." She stands, snapping the waistband of my pants as she goes. With her eyes latched on mine, I lift my hips and she tugs, slipping them down my legs and then tossing them to the floor. I suck in a breath when she palms me, cupping me and pressing her thumb against the sensitive pad beneath my crown. Pleasure ripples across my stomach. She holds my gaze while shimmying out of her shorts. Shit. My heart thuds as she climbs up, a knee on either side of my thighs.

"Ari," I moan through the feeling of her moving against me.

"I want to make you come, Jesse Carroway."

I nod, licking my lips. "I'm pretty sure those are the best words ever strung together in the history of the English language."

She laughs, but it's short and choked off when she rocks her hips, moving enough to spread her open and for me to slide right in.

At the first full pass, we both moan. I lose my shit the second time and grab her hips, helping to direct pace and motion. And oh fuck, looking at me through long lashes, Ariana sheds fear like a cloak, dropping it to the floor as she pulls the pins from her hair and shakes it out. All that's left is a carnal, ripe woman falling apart above me. I can do nothing but focus on the slick, wet heat surrounding me. And when she touches her lips to mine, open and breathing in the same breath I pant out, I lose my mind.

I lose all sense of self and time, and any distance between us is destroyed with each grunt and groan. I jab my hips up to meet the press of hers, just as the tip of my tongue reaches into her mouth to strangle the sounds driven from her with each stroke. The chair rocks beneath us. I shift lower, providing more room for her to move.

She bucks against me, frantic and sinking her nails into my shoulders, dragging them into my hair as she arches and groans for more and faster, please.

I give it to her. I'd give her anything. I'll give her my everything.

I bite the swell of her breast and then find the tip, sucking it through the cotton of her tank. She squeals and jerks her hips harder, grinding down on me so brutally, I see stars, and I'm nothing but an aching knot of need.

She whimpers, and the last ribbon of my control is cut.

"Come right now, Ari," I order.

I grab her hair, pulling her forehead to mine while I move faster. A strangled cry erupts from her trembling lips as her body grows taut, straining over me for a long moment. And then she breaks, crying out. I keep going, though, keep stroking against her, seeing her through violent lashes that leave her trembling and clinging to my neck.

"Yes." I press the word into the sweet spot behind her ear, dragging in the scent of her. Surrounded by Ariana, the only woman who I've ever loved...will ever love, I grind my eyes closed and I come. I come so fucking hard, every muscle in my body tightens like I'm having a heart attack.

Holy shit. I can't even think with this woman, this damn woman. I lose control every single time.

I'll need a brain transplant to recover if she ever leaves me.

I return to reality when her tongue traces the lines of the tattoos covering my chest.

I grab her hair and haul her face up to catch her eyes sparkling from mischief in the overhead light.

She smiles. She smiles that damn smile that tightens my chest, and I can't breathe.

"I love you, Jesse."

I kiss her. I drown in her. I take from her, and I see light and something new.

19
NOW

ARIANA

Tonight is my first performance by myself. We had done a few promotional appearances with the guys, where I sang a few songs with them. I recorded a single with Tanner, Jensen, and Jesse, but the single Jesse and I recorded was going to be on *their* next album so my album wasn't all The Sound of Us. My first single with Tanner is still reigning supreme on the Billboard charts and the crowds have gotten bigger and bigger at each performance. Clark's strategy is to release my album like the Chainsmokers, with a song or two released every couple of weeks, and the whole album released at the end. We released my second single, "Wreckage", last Friday and it was starting to move up the charts as well.

Yes, my past performances had gone well. But I wasn't sure how a performance would go where it was just me. Clark had been giving me pep talks all day, but they couldn't quench the fear that I was going to go out there and there would be crickets.

Tonight, I'm the first opening act for Red Daydreams and

I'm just hoping that there's some crossover between their fans and people who would like me... or this is going to be an interesting performance.

I'm getting my makeup done when there's a knock on the door. "Come in," I call out, and one of Red Daydream's assistants is standing there with a snotty look on his face. I'm distracted from his attitude though, by the giant bouquet of roses that he's holding in his arms.

"This came for you," he says haughtily, obviously pissed about having to help the opening act. He leaves without another word.

I feel a sense of dread as I look at the flowers.

"Those are beautiful," gushes Ellie, my makeup artist, as we both stare at them. "You're a lucky girl."

I know she thinks they must be from the guys. My relationship with them has become the worst kept secret ever after that interview in New York.

But I know it's not from them. They would never send me roses. Not when they know that Gentry always got me roses.

I stand up, ignoring the fact that Ellie isn't done with my eye makeup yet, and I walk over to the flowers. My breathing sounds shallow in my ears as I look at the tag with shaking hands.

Kick Ass Tonight
-Clark

I stagger back a little in relief, and then I just feel silly. Of course, it's not Gentry. My security team would have checked before the flowers got back here.

After relief comes anger that I had that reaction at all. I wonder if there will be a day where I'm not haunted by him.

I'm also going to find a way to suggest that Clark never send me roses again.

"Who was it from?" Ellie asks eagerly.

"Clark," I tell her, trying to look normal and not like I just freaked out.

"Okayyy," she says, gesturing for me to sit back down with a tight smile. I must have looked a little crazy when I responded, because she doesn't look at ease anymore.

After a few minutes, she clears her throat. "So, you and Clark seem really close," she remarks, trying to make her statement seem innocent.

I shoot her a glance, knowing exactly what she's thinking...that Clark and I are having an affair or something like that.

"He's a good manager," I say politely, not really caring to defend myself from her way off base thoughts.

I'm about to say something else, when there's a knock on the door again. "Come in," I say, less confidently this time.

This time, when the same surly employee appears in the doorway, I'm not nervous. Because I know that the gift he has in his hands is definitely not from Gentry.

Ellie starts laughing, and I start laughing too, because my "gift" is a lifesize cardboard cutout of Tanner. There's a post-it-note on the chest of the cardboard Tanner that says "for your good luck kiss."

I want to cry at the gesture. This is probably my favorite gift I've ever received.

Elle is gushing, but I can't hear what she's saying because I'm already eagerly calling Tanner.

My insides seem to take flight when he picks up, and I hear his gravelly voice that will forever remind me of sex.

"Princess," he says in an amused tone.

"I love you," I tell him immediately, ignoring the fact that Ellie seems like she's about to pass out from watching me.

"I love you too," he says quietly. "Tonight is going to be perfect," he continues with complete confidence.

And just like that, my nerves die down. Sometimes all you need is for one person to believe in you.

I'm about to say something...because there are a million words we haven't said lately, but the employee is back again, this time not bothering to knock on the door.

"You're up in five," he calls out, looking annoyed that I'd dare be on the phone.

"Talk to you later?" I ask, and he hums in agreement.

"Okay," I whisper.

"Okay, then."

"Bye Tanner." And then I hang up.

"I guess you're not sleeping with your manager, then," Ellie says, and I just look at her with one eyebrow raised.

She blushes, finally realizing that she's overstepped, and I walk out of the room to prepare to go on stage.

I'm hustled to the side of the stage by one of the backstage managers.

This is it. This is what I've been wanting for so long that it seems like forever.

I step out to the stage. The arena is only half full, which is honestly more than I expected, since people usually arrive late to concerts when there are multiple opening acts like this one.

I get a polite round of applause when I introduce myself, and then I start. I only get to sing five songs tonight, so I've chosen my single with Tanner (Tanner's part will be sung by one of Red Daydream's backup singers), three of my songs, and then a cover of Halsey's "Finally // beautiful stranger," a song that will forever remind me of the guys.

I'm singing "Wreckage," when I look out in the crowd and I see a teenage girl whose belting my song back at me with all of her heart. She knows every word. And the sight almost makes me cry. Because I never in a million years thought I would see it.

I once read an article about a famous pop star, and during the interview she talked about how there was no greater moment than when the crowd starts singing your song back to you, and you just know that what you wrote actually means something to them.

I don't take my eyes off that girl for the rest of the song, and her smile lights up her whole face as she continues to sing.

And I know that no matter what happens with the rest of my performances; this moment will stand out like a burning flame in my mind. A memory that I'll treasure for as long as I live.

For so long my songs have been my little secret. The story of a life that I've never wanted to live. A story of broken dreams, and broken things.

And I know that this one fan gets that.

And it's all worth it.

The rest of the songs go off without a hitch, and the crowd has actually grown as I go through all my songs. I'm riding high as I run off stage, and after accepting congratulations from a few members of Red Daydream, I head back to my dressing room to call the guys before their performance.

When I walk in, I let out a small scream. Because the room has been trashed, and the Tanner cutout has been slashed to pieces. My bodyguards come running in, and it's emergency protocol as soon as they see the state of the dressing room.

I'm immediately dragged outside into a waiting vehicle by two of them and whisked back to the hotel we're staying at tonight.

I know without anyone telling me that Gentry was here. And I'm sick to my stomach that instead of calling and telling the guys about how amazing the show is, I'll have to answer questions about Gentry instead.

It's just another moment that he's stolen from me.

Our Facetime call goes as I expect. Jensen tries to order me to call off the tour for now...which obviously isn't going to happen, Tanner goes quiet-even more than usual-and Jesse tries to smooth everything over. It's the same song and dance that's been happening since even before I was shot, and I'm so tired of it.

The next few weeks start to run together. I'm performing and then I'm traveling either to see the guys or to the next stop. They pop up in between their tour dates as well, but the pressure of everything is tearing at our seams and I feel like I'm barely holding onto them.

And at every performance no matter what measures are taken, there's always a nasty surprise from Gentry.

A picture of the two of us...or a note...or even my wedding veil. They appear randomly, brought by different people or put in places that I can't miss.

I never see Gentry, and that's almost worse. The waiting for the big reveal.

I'm losing weight, and my nightmares are constant.

But there are more and more fans who are singing my songs back to me every night.

And somehow, that makes me push through the fact that my ex is stalking me, and the guys are fighting with me.

The only time I feel alive is on the stage.

And I can't help but think that the worst is yet to come.

20
THEN

ARIANA

"I've been looking for you," Tanner says quietly, and I'm not surprised that he's found me.

I didn't follow the guys in to the house this morning. Instead, I set off down the road, ignoring their calls until I could get a cab.

And even though I couldn't afford it, I had that cab take me all the way to the beach house. For some reason, I only associated good things with it, and I really needed to think of good things right now.

"Why are you here?" I ask quietly, not looking at him, even as he walks closer towards me.

He's suddenly in front of me, and I close my eyes.

"You see me when no one else does. And, Ari, I see you too," he tells me. He drops a kiss on both my eyelids. "These eyes see things most of us miss and are the windows to every single one of your thoughts." He presses our foreheads together. "I'm sorry I hurt you last night."

My heart races so hard, but I can't speak, my throat is

clogged with emotion. No one has ever spoken to me like this.

"And these lips, that fucking freckle. They're a work of art I can't imagine not kissing for the rest of my life."

I lean forward and press my mouth to his against my better judgment. His lips are beautiful, too. They've got a deep bow on the top and are full and lush on the bottom, and I've daydreamed about kissing them all day at school since I met him.

He groans and cups my face with both hands, holds me there, and kisses me like he's in pain, and I'm the only drug that can cure him.

I thought I knew what it would feel like to kiss all of them. But it changed every time we did kiss.

This kiss…Tanner's kiss… It feels like coming home and going on an adventure all at once. Safe and reckless. Weightless, but so firmly rooted to this moment. And when he runs his tongue over my lips, I open for him.

"So fucking perfect," he murmurs before his warm tongue slides into my mouth. I moan and slide closer to him until I'm nearly in his lap. I clutch at the front of his shirt and hold on while his mouth shows mine what a kiss is supposed to feel like. Behind my eyes, a million points of brilliant light explode, and I hurtle through time, space, and at the same time, I remain grounded, held in place by the gravity of his kiss. I feel this kiss all the way to my toes, filling up the empty spaces in a way that I never dreamed was possible.

And I know I'll never forget it.

His hands grab my waist, and he lifts me up and puts me down so I'm straddling him. And the kiss changes. It's feverish, my hands go from clutching to tugging, his hips ruck up into me, his erection presses against the softest, hottest part of me, and I start to ache.

"Tanner—" I break the kiss and try to catch my breath.

"I need more," he growls and his lips drag across my jaw, sucking and biting. I whimper, sigh, and hold on for dear life.

Suddenly, I break our kiss and push away from him as a kaleidoscope of images run through my brain of last night. I shouldn't be kissing him like this.

Tanner grimaces when he sees the look on my face.

I blink to clear my eyes and struggle to catch my breath. His chest heaves, too. We gaze at each other, neither one of us smiling.

"Can I take you out this weekend to apologize?" he asks, his voice is low, urgent, and his eyes are hooded with desire.

"I don't know," I reply, still looking at him, realizing that this beautiful, flawed boy really knows nothing about me at all.

"There's a song," I say softly to him, my eyes flickering out to the waves crashing against the beach. I look back at him, and I watch as the heat fades from his gaze as he concentrates on what I'm saying. "I can't remember who the song's by. But I remember that the singer talks about loving in shades of wrong. That phrase has always stuck with me."

I pause and just keep looking at him, memorizing the way the failing light of the day looks on him at this moment.

"What if that's how I love? What if that's how we love? And what if it's all wrong?" I ask, desperate for him to tell me that my fear isn't real.

He doesn't have an answer for me, and maybe that's an answer in itself.

21
NOW

ARIANA

I can fully admit that I have a problem as I walk through the hotel lobby to surprise the guys. They weren't expecting me until tomorrow but it's Tanner's birthday today and with everything that's been happening lately, I'm just trying to keep us all going. When there happened to be a flight available after my meeting in New York City, I knew I had to take it. Tanner hates birthdays, and I'm the only one who knows that.

No matter what was going on though, ultimately, they were my home. Complicated or not, I couldn't spend too much time away from them without feeling a burning need inside of me to return.

I just wondered if they still felt the same way about seeing me.

"I need a key for Judd Cavanaugh's room," I tell the front desk, using the pseudonym that the guys used most often when they were in hotels.

"And you are…?" he asks, looking at me distrustingly.

"Snow White," I say with a small grin. It was the codename that the boys decided on. I didn't have seven men, but they felt like three was close enough. This was the first time I was having to use it, since in the past, I'd always been with them. Using the name helps me shake off some nerves and the general sense of uneasiness I've had for some reason since walking into the hotel.

The employee looks down at the computer again, his face annoyed. A look of surprise crosses his face. He must've seen "Snow White" on the list. When he looks up at me again, all the suspicion is wiped from his face. It's replaced with a look of simpering respect and calculation that I've seen in a lot of people's eyes when they found out I was involved with the band. I'm sure he's wondering, beneath his beady little eyes, what my connection is with them and what I can do for him.

"The key. I only have a few hours," I say to him, immediately realizing what that sounded like after it left my mouth.

His weaselly grin only widens. I roll my eyes.

It takes another five minutes before I have the key in my hand. He handed it to me in that little key folder that hotels always give out. I open it up as I'm going up the elevator and I'm not surprised to see his number and a note to "call Wesley for a good time" written inside. I highly doubt that Wesley can give anyone a good time.

It's early in the morning, and I don't expect any of the guys to be up, considering they had a show last night. It was really hard that I missed the show, since we had been taking turns flying back and forth to see each other perform. At the start of our tours, we'd had a 48-hour rule for the amount of time we could be apart. But eventually, it had become too hard on all of us to keep up with that, and Clark started sending me to more promotional events in between shows. This wasn't the first time I hadn't come back when I was supposed to, and I knew that at least Tanner was getting more and more upset about it.

A flash of guilt creeps into my mind. For not the first time,

I wonder if we all can have our dreams for our career *and* make the relationship work.

I shove the thought off. Hopefully, I would get big enough that the record label would be interested in me opening for the guys next, and then we'd always be together. Who knows, maybe someday they'd be opening for me... or at least we'd be headlining together.

At least that was my dream.

Wesley gave me three keys for some reason. I thought it was strange that the guys weren't staying in one suite together, like we had when I was traveling with them. I guess they just needed space?

I didn't know who was staying where, so I just knocked on the first door that I came to. A minute passes and no one answers. I'm about to try another room, when the door creaks open and an exhausted looking Jesse appears. His blonde hair is sticking up everywhere, and he looks like he had a rough night. I guess the after party was intense. A wave of unease passes over me, and I have to actively push it away. I trust them. I do. But we don't really do afterparties when I'm with them, and the few times I did attend it was definitely not my favorite thing between the groupies and the out of control roadies.

"Ari?" he asks, a big smile lighting up his face as he scoops me into his arms and begins peppering my face with kisses. "You're early," he says, stating the obvious.

"Is that alright?" I ask, suddenly feeling a bit self-conscious.

He looks at me like I'm crazy. "You're joking, right? I'm always having to resist the urge to come kidnap you from your tour and keep you by my side, always. Or just quit the band and become your kept boytoy," he says with a wink.

The laugh that comes out of me is just what I need, and whatever weird feeling I just had dissipates. "Where's Jensen and Tanner?" I ask, looking into Jesse's room and seeing that it's empty.

Jesse rolls his eyes. "Jensen needed some space," he says, making me laugh again at the way that he says it, like he and Jensen are in a relationship and taking a break.

"And Tanner...is Tanner," he explains vaguely before grabbing his key card off the table next to the door and walking out with me. "Let's go see if birthday boy is still alive after last night."

"Was it a big party?" I ask nonchalantly, trying to act as if I don't care.

He looks at me knowingly. And then a look of concern crosses his face. "Tanner's been going a little hard lately," he says in a concerned voice.

"We've been seeing each other every few days," I respond crossly. "How have I not known this? And what do you mean by hard? Do you think he's..." I begin to ask, dread curling in my gut.

Jesse grimaces. "Perhaps," he admits, making my jaw drop. "But you don't need to worry," he hurriedly adds. "Jensen and I are watching him. If it gets too out of hand, we'll handle it. You really don't need to worry. You've got enough on your plate," he says.

"You really think he's doing drugs again?" I ask, wringing my hands. "Maybe I should just take a break."

"No," Jesse says harshly. "You're not gonna give up your dream just because one of your boyfriends is acting like a douche," he says. "And besides, we haven't actually seen him doing it. I just suspect it, but I could be totally wrong. Tanner's been completely clean since you came back into our lives."

I hear the things in Jesse's voice that he doesn't say. That I'm not exactly "in" their lives at the moment. Which isn't fair at all.

But I let it go for now.

"I'm sure it's fine, let's go wake him up and start the birthday celebrations…or I guess continue them," he says, frowning as he thinks about whatever happened last night.

I nod, my stomach clenching. We walk down the hall, and I think again of the separate rooms. "How often have you guys been getting separate rooms? It's never like this when I come," I remark.

Jesse pauses, clearly not wanting to answer my question.

"We've just all been a little tense. Kinda getting tired of life on the road," he says. Again, I can read the words that he isn't saying.

Everything is falling apart because I'm not here.

I let it go though, because what could I say? Sorry for actually doing something for myself for once in my life?

Yeah, that didn't seem like something I should apologize for.

We knock on the door, even though Jesse has a key to the room, but no one answers. I can hear the faint pulsing of music coming from beyond the door.

After a minute, Jesse finally swipes the key when no one answers.

As soon as we walk in, I just know that something is wrong. Tanner's staying in a suite, the suite that the guys would usually stay in all together because it has three bedrooms. And the place is trashed. It's not just trashed, it's demolished. There are people passed out all over. Some are half clothed, and some are even naked.

There's a hole in the wall. Lamps are knocked over. Beer bottles, empty liquor bottles, food… It's everywhere. I almost step in some vomit until Jesse pulls me out of the way. I don't see Tanner's body strewn on the floor though, and I'm not sure if that's a good thing. He's not in the first or second bedroom either.

"Maybe let me go in there first," Jesse says as we approach the third door.

"He wouldn't," I tell him, trying to assure both of us, but Jesse doesn't reply.

I let him open the door anyway.

Whatever he sees isn't good, because he quickly backs out. "He doesn't look like he's in good shape. Why don't we go eat breakfast and he can meet us later?" he says.

And I know then that whatever's in that room is going to change things.

I push him gently to the side, and I walk in.

I immediately want to cry, throw up, rage against the world. He's ruined everything. This wasn't supposed to happen in love stories. Especially not ours. We've been through too much for this to happen.

But the proof is right in front of me. It really is happening.

Tanner's lying in an unmade bed, on his stomach, naked. That would ordinarily not be cause for concern, since Tanner always sleeps naked. But there's an equally naked girl lying next to him. Her arm is strewn across his back.

Jesse is trying to get me out of the room, but I'm frozen.

Tanner must hear the commotion, because he flips over to his back. He opens his eyes, and just looks at me, and there's acceptance and resignation in his gaze, like he knows it's all ruined.

My eyes flick away from him and dance across the room. There's a small pile of white powder on the dresser next to him that I'm just now noticing. We both see it at the same time, but Tanner's face doesn't change. The blonde groans just then, and Tanner finally starts to look sick.

He looks over at her, and his face is haunted.

"Princess," he finally says.

But I cut him off. "Don't you dare," I hiss at him. "Don't you dare say this isn't what it looks like," I say as I begin to back away.

Just then, the vomit that I've been trying to keep in splatters out, peppering the already dirty floor with the remnants of the breakfast sandwich I had at the airport this morning. Jesse puts his arms around me just then and starts to help me back out of the room, because it's like I'm having an out of body experience at the moment.

Tanner's off the bed, completely naked, trying to come after me. Jesse pushes me behind him and cuts off Tanner before he can get any closer.

"Leave her alone," Jesse growls at him, so different from his usual easy-going attitude. Tanner's sobbing now, big ugly sobs that sound strange coming from this man that I've almost never seen cry.

He starts to beg me to listen to him, beg me to give him a chance. He looks broken, his face scrunched up in pain so tangible that I can almost taste it. It mirrors my own pain. I turn around to run and escape it, and instead, I run right into Jensen, who has just appeared behind me.

"What's going on, Ari?" he says, his face a mix of confusion and joy at seeing me.

"Where have you been?" I growl through my tears, and the confusion on his face only grows.

"I have my own room just like Jesse, why?" he asks. But then his eyes take in the scene in front of him. The blonde wanders out now, still naked as the day she was born, jutting her breasts out proudly as she puts her arms around Tanner's waist.

And I can't be there anymore. I run out of the room, stepping on a few passed out people as I go.

I thought I had already been through the worst there was.

But I never saw this coming.

And I just wonder that after surviving David and then Gentry...how I'll ever survive this.

I'm huddled in a hotel room that I booked as soon as I left Tanner's room, trying to arrange for a flight back early. I feel bad, because Jesse and Jensen have been trying to call me since they don't know where I am, but I'm just not in the mood to see any of them right now.

A knock sounds on the door. And somehow, I know that it's Tanner. I can practically feel his guilt and anguish permeating through the door. For a second, I debate not answering, but eventually, I decide it's best to just get it over with. I have no idea if he's going to grovel or try to make excuses. But either way I need to be done with Tanner Crosby after this.

I take a deep breath, and I walk shakily to the door. Opening it up, I can see that I was right. Standing there-pale, tired, and awful looking-is Tanner.

Now that I'm examining him closely, I can see that he looks like he's lost weight since the last time I saw him, which was only two weeks ago. He's lost at least ten pounds. I wonder if that's because of the drugs.

Or maybe he's been "working out" more, I comment sarcastically to myself, thinking of the blonde again.

He clears his throat, like he's about to throw up at my feet. "Hi," he finally says in a choked voice.

I simply stare at him silently, and open up the door to let him in.

"It's nice that you were able to take a break," he says awkwardly. I look at him incredulously, not sure what he's trying to do. "Listen, I just came by because I wanted to tell you to not take this out on Jesse and Jensen. They haven't done anything wrong. I'm the fuck up here. They haven't partied at all since you left, haven't even really talked to other girls unless they're forced to at signing events," he says.

"That's what you came here to say?" I ask in a shaky voice. I want him to tell me I just imagined everything. I want him to beg me for a second chance.

I've been in love with this silver eyed boy since I knew

what love was. I don't know how to just let that go. I don't know how he can just let it go.

He starts to walk to the door, and I realize that he has nothing else to say. I'm crying now, silent tears that stream down my face. They're a mix of heartbreak and anger, because how can one emotion outweigh the other right now?

I would have followed this boy anywhere. I have followed him, down all the dark paths his heart has taken us. I've dragged him into the light, even when it took something away from me to do it. He came to me broken, and I've spent years of my life trying to put back the parts that were missing from him.

My love for him has always burned hot and wild, and now that we're at this moment, I can't help but think I should have known.

I've always taken Tanner's demons, and thought I had to make them mine.

And that was never going to end well.

But if this is our last goodbye, I just want someone to tell me who I'm supposed to be if I can't love him anymore.

Tanner hesitates at the door. He looks back at me over his shoulder. I can see that his silver eyes are shiny with tears, but I wish there were more. I wish he was on the floor right now, shattering into pieces, because that's how I feel.

"I just want you to know how sorry I am, Ari. I'm so fucking sorry," he whispers before leaving the room.

I fall to my knees. I can't breathe. I didn't know a heart could feel like this and still live. I'd never known that pain could be so silent, and yet, so loud.

But now I do.

I give myself an hour, and then I leave on my flight.

I've had several new beginnings over the course of my life.

But this doesn't feel like a fresh start.

It feels like the very end.

Tanner

I'm a fucking loser. I've always known it, and now she knows it too. No matter how much she tried to save me, nothing she did ever worked. Because I needed to want to save myself. And I didn't know how to do that.

I pull out the flask that's ever present in my pocket and drink it down, savoring the sharp bite of whiskey as it goes down my throat. I then walk to my suitcase, and dig to the bottom of it until I get to the Altoids container that really holds my stash of Percocet. I swallow five of them down, wishing that my stash of coke wasn't gone.

I need something to make me forget.

I hadn't fucked that girl. After Ari stepped back into our lives, my dick couldn't make an appearance for anyone but her. She had always been it for me. But the opportunity that I hadn't known I'd been waiting for was too perfect to pass up.

Ari, deserved better than me. I would only drag her down, because I couldn't stop my demons from dragging me under. Even if I got clean again, checked myself into rehab for the fourth time, I wouldn't be able to stop. I was weak, where she was strong. I wasn't going to do that to her.

So I let her believe that I fucked that girl. I had her security team keeping me updated on every move she made so I knew she was coming early today for my birthday. When I woke up this morning and saw what I had done to myself, how pathetic I was-lying in a pool of vomit-I couldn't take Ari being around me anymore.

When that girl walked in my room this morning and tried to get into bed with me, I took the opportunity to make sure Ari finally let me go. She had only been in my bed for a minute, but a minute was all it took.

And even then, I almost messed it all up by running after her, my very soul begging me not to push her away.

I would break her heart now, so that it wouldn't break worse in the future when I inevitably let her down for the millionth time, and she realized that she had wasted her life on a broken man.

I'm lost in dark thoughts when the door crashes open and an irate Jensen is standing there. "You stupid, fucking asshole," he growls at me, striding over to grab me by the collar of my shirt, shaking me so hard that my teeth clack together.

"Why did you do this?" he asks, the end of his sentence coming out pained rather than angry. I know he's hurting too. Both he and Jesse are hurting. They love her, and they love me. And I've destroyed the only real family I've ever had.

"This is for the best," I tell him. He lets me go, disgusted. Staring at my eyes, I know he can see how dilated they are, how high I'm getting right now as the pills and alcohol begin to take effect.

"You're unbelievable. You just lost the girl you've been obsessed with for forever, and you're getting high right now instead of going after her."

He shakes his head in disgust and points his finger at me as he walks towards the door. "If you fucked things up for Jesse and I, I will never forgive you. If you don't make this right, we're done."

He doesn't bother to find out my answer, as he's out the door, slamming it behind him. I can hear him screaming at all the leftover party guests that they need to get the fuck out.

I dig for more pills, and I lay down on my bed that stinks of alcohol and the heavy perfume of that chick.

It's for the best, I tell myself as I fade into a nightmare filled sleep.

It's for the best.

22
THEN

ARIANA

Tanner is in a mood. He'd been quiet all night. I knew that his dad had been in town this week for a business deal, and that was most likely to blame, but I hated when he got like this.

Even at the show they played earlier, he had been subdued, his energy on stage lacking that passion that he usually possessed in spades. Jesse and Jensen were looking at each other furtively as we sit at the after-party. For once, it's at someone's house besides Tanner's. Jesse catches my attention and lifts his chin at me before nodding his head towards Tanner. I get the message.

My relationship with Tanner… is different than with the others. Once I broke through Jensen's wall, and especially after the death of his mom, he doesn't hide who he is anymore. And Jesse has always been open with me, pursuing me with abandon, there hasn't been a moment where he made me doubt what he wanted. Jesse was real.

Tanner is a whole other story, though. It's always two steps forward, one step back with him. Sometimes I get glimpses of the real Tanner, but as soon as he sees that I'm looking and that I'm actually seeing him, he shuts down. So I'm not sure exactly how to approach this.

"We should go get snow cones," I say suddenly, knowing that Tanner loves the stuff. Jesse and Jensen roll their eyes at me with matching smirks. Tanner's so lost in his thoughts though, he totally misses what I'm trying to do.

He stares at me for a moment as if he's coming out of a daze. "I could go for some," he finally says, and I give myself an inner high-five.

We get up to go, but Jesse and Jensen stay seated. Tanner throws them an inquiring look.

"You guys go, I have a game of beer pong calling my name," Jensen stands up and stretches, showcasing a couple of inches of golden skin as his shirt moves up with the movement. Just that peek has my mouth watering.

"I think I'm going to join him," Jesse says. "You guys go ahead. We'll meet up with you later."

Tanner looks nonplussed about the fact that it will just be me and him, but I'm nervous as hell. We begin to walk through the ever-growing crowd, but Tanner surprises me by reaching out and grabbing my hand. I look up at him quickly, but he isn't looking at me, he's trying to avoid all the people that are trying to get his attention. We make it outside, and the humidity feels even worse than usual. There's supposed to be a storm soon, and the air feels so thick it almost feels like I'm wading through it to get to Tanner's car.

While Jesse and Jensen's cars are both very expensive, Tanner's car puts them to shame. I've heard guys at school practically gushing about how there's only a couple of these cars made in the world. Slipping into the smooth leather interior and staring at the dashboard that resembles a computer, I'm more aware than ever of the differences between the guys and myself.

We start driving, not exchanging any words. Finally, I

open my mouth to try and pierce the sudden tension that I'm feeling.

"Where's your favorite snow cone place?" I ask, only knowing about a few that are nowhere near where we are right now.

"It's just a mile from here," he says, not offering anything else. We don't speak until we get there. And then it's just for him to ask me what we want as we pull through the drive through.

We eat our snow cones in silence as he drives, and I realize that we're going to the beach house. He parks, and we sit there for a second before he gets out and starts walking out to the beach without a word.

I get out of the car and follow at a distance.

He doesn't stop walking until the waves are licking at his feet. You can't see the stars or the moon because of the storm, and the beach is only faintly lit from a few lights on the property next to us.

He's standing there, facing the ocean, his shoulders hunched over, his posture broken looking.

I watch him for a moment before I decide to check on him. People say that they want to be alone, but no one ever really wants that when they're hurting. And it's obvious that Tanner is hurting badly.

"Tanner," I whisper, and he stiffens like he'd forgotten that I was with him.

"Do you ever just wish you could disappear?" he asks.

I don't answer, knowing somehow that I just need to listen.

"Sometimes I think about what it would be like just to get swept out to sea. I once got caught in a wave when I was a little boy, and I remember floating in the water, not sure whether someone was going to save me. All I could see was the sky, and it got smaller and smaller as I began to sink. And

I just remember having a peaceful feeling, like no matter what, it was going to be okay."

He sighs and I continue to be silent even though I'm itching to wrap him in my arms.

"I think that eventually, it will all be too much. And I just think sometimes that I would do anything to feel that moment of peace, just one more time."

I feel like I'm a coward right now, because here he is showing me his truth, and I'm not showing him any of my scars. I can't even speak.

He laughs just then, a hollow sound. "You feel that way, don't you, Princess?" he says, looking down at me with those uncanny silver eyes.

I look at him in surprise.

"You and me, we're the same. I just don't wear my scars on the outside," I admit to him in a murmur that can barely be heard over the waves crashing against our feet.

"You can definitely see my scars," he answers, looking back at the water. And I hold my breath, because I just know that he's about to tell me something important.

"My dad was so fucking proud when he found out that he was having a son. He didn't even care when I came out with eyes that were nothing like his or my mother's. I was everything to him. The next heir of the Crosby fortune. But he went in for some testing when I was five. And he found out that he was shooting blanks. He confronted my mother, and she tried to deny it at first. And I wondered why my mother and I were both thrown out into the front yard in the middle of the night."

A large wave crashes against the shore, spraying us with water, but he doesn't even seem to notice.

"She banged on that door for hours, begging to be let back in. She feared being poor more than she feared being miserable. He finally let us back in, but my life changed that night."

He pointed to a cross tattoo on his arm that said: "Only God can judge me."

"This hides the three-inch scar I got that next day, when he threw me down the stairs. And this hides the scar where he sliced me with a hunting knife," he explains, pointing to a rose that looks like it's dripping blood.

I shiver, feeling sick as he talks.

"Almost every time he comes home, he carves out a piece of me. And I can't do fucking anything, because he'll kill my mother if I do. I've given up eighteen fucking years for her, and she couldn't care less. So when I walk away, that will be it. She'll be on her own, just like I've been all these years."

I don't say anything, I just wrap my arms around him and try to give him my love. And I can't help but think of what a pair we are. Both fighting our own demons. And I wonder if it's only a matter of time until we both crash and burn.

Because I don't think I can save him when I can't even save myself.

23
NOW

ARIANA

"How are you doing?" Clark asks when he sees me at my next show. He doesn't know about what happened, and I've tried to keep it that way since he represents both of us.

"I'm fine," I lie. It's all I can say, because the real answer is that I've been destroyed and I don't know how to fix myself.

That seems to be a good enough response for him, because he pulls a large packing envelope out of the briefcase he has with him.

"What's going on?" I ask. Clark just smiles and hands me the envelope. I open it, and my hands start shaking. It's my album cover. I took the shots a few weeks ago and picked the cover myself, but seeing it on an actual album was unreal. In the shot, I'm lying on a grassy field, the stars stretched out before me with the album name written in the stars. You could see that I was holding someone's hand in the shot, but you couldn't see who the hand belonged to. I smiled because it was Jesse's hand in the shot of course, because I couldn't stargaze without him.

Just as I smile, my heart clenches at the fact that I haven't really talked to Jesse or Jensen since I left the hotel. We've exchanged texts, but I've been too raw to talk to them on the phone. I know they will want to talk about what happened, and I just can't do that right now.

The next couple of weeks, I go through the motions. But I'm just empty inside. I'm once again letting a man mess with my hopes and dreams, but I can't help it.

It's Tanner.

I ache inside and although time is passing, I'm not healing at all. If anything, the hole inside of me is growing even wider. And I wonder if anything I'm doing is even worth it, if I'm doing it all alone.

I can't seem to fix what's broken between Jesse and Jensen either, because I can't help but think, what if they're next? What if I'm just not enough? Or the pressures of family, Tanner, me being away… It just all becomes too much?

If you asked me two weeks ago if I thought it was possible for any of them to ever cheat on me, I would've said no. Yet here we are. Maybe it was unrealistic for me to think that we could last in the first place.

Not that I would ever give someone an excuse to cheat, but maybe the whole reality of this relationship working was idealistic. I mean, I was dating three men and expecting them not to date anyone else.

Either way, everything sucks.

Clark confronts me after the show tonight. "What the hell, Ari?" he snaps at me. "I give you this opportunity, and that's the best you have to offer?" he says angrily. And I don't blame him. I sucked tonight. I even started crying while I was singing Tanner's and my single.

"I'm going through some personal things at the moment" I tell him not looking him in the eye.

"Let me guess, you're having trouble with my other clients," he says dryly.

I shrug my shoulders, even though I really just want to talk to someone about how my life has fallen apart.

Clark comes and sits down next to me with a sigh. "Let me give you a piece of advice, Ariana," he begins. "This is your chance. Chances like this are once-in-a-lifetime, and Jesse, Jensen, and Tanner...they already got their chance. And they took it. And they succeeded. And they have their careers. And as much as they love you and want what I assume is what's best for you, they're never going to care about your dream as much as you care about it. I don't know all the history with your ex, but it sounds like you spent a large portion of your life living for other people. This is your chance to live for you, and who knows, maybe the life that you build doing this for yourself makes everything with them even better."

He takes a deep breath and then stands up. "Take a few days off and come back with your head on straight." And I can hear the implication in his voice. Don't bother coming back if you can't fix yourself is what he really means.

Sitting there, I know he's right. I may be heartbroken. But giving up on myself and my dreams will only make everything worse.

I can't go on like this.

Not giving myself time to think, I pick up my phone and called Amberlie.

"Ari?" she says sleepily when she picks up, and I wince, knowing that she probably had gone to bed since she usually has to be up super early to teach her class.

"It's me," I tell her, and my voice is already breaking despite the little pep talk I had just given myself.

She's instantly alert. "Is everything okay?" she asks me, her voice full of worry.

I say a silent prayer of thanks that she's back in my life. She had been an amazing friend in high school, the best you could have hoped for. And the fact that she had no problem picking right back up after I ditched her for so many years...that made her priceless.

"I'm in San Antonio," I tell her.

"Did you just finish a show?" she asks, her voice filled with pride at my accomplishments.

"I did," I say, trying to keep my voice level. "I was wondering if you wanted to go on a girls' trip with me," I blurt out.

Now she sounds really awake. "Of course. When?"

I grimace, wondering how feasible it is to even find a substitute teacher with so little time. "I was wondering if we could go this week," I say softly. "I'll pay for your flight and everything. Do you think there's any way that you can get off?"

"I can pay for myself, but just tell me where to fly," she squeals. "The kids have been little monsters this month, and I haven't taken any time off all year yet. I know that Teddy won't have a problem watching Cody by himself for a few days. He's always saying how I deserve to have a break."

Not for the first time I think about how happy I am-and a little jealous-about the life my friend has managed to build for herself.

"I'll pay for the flight, no arguing," I tell her. "And I was thinking Scottsdale."

She squeals and begins to talk about how she once went to Scottsdale with a rich aunt and all the good shopping there. And it feels strange to listen to her, because how can she be so happy when my life has fallen apart?

It was weird how the human existence worked like that. We were all connected, and yet so far apart at the same time.

"I'll send the flight details if Wednesday works for you," I finally tell her after she's finished telling her story.

We exchange goodbyes, and I get online, buy the tickets, and then send her the information.

Maybe a few days in the sun can help, I think hopefully.

But I know that it's just wishful thinking, because nothing is going to make my heart stop hurting.

It's hot when we land in Scottsdale, and that's an understatement. The dryness is refreshing though, since the last couple of shows in Texas were so humid that it was almost unbearable.

Amberlie's waiting in the baggage claim when I walk out, and she squeals and runs over to give me a huge hug. I have a ballcap pulled down low on my head, just because people are starting to occasionally recognize me and I don't feel like talking to anyone.

"Thanks for giving me a much needed break from those hellions," she says as she flips her hair out of her face.

"Always happy to help," I say as I try to laugh at her exuberance. I fail miserably though, and Amberlie obviously notices it, because she gets a concerned look on her face. My face starts to crumble, and she pulls me in for another hug.

"Oh, honey," she soothes. "We'll talk all about it, but let's get to our hotel first," she says, eyeing the people around us.

I straighten up and try to school my face. I wasn't anyone big yet, but there was always the chance that someone had seen the headlines of the shooting and hints about my relationship with the guys. That's all I needed was a picture to go up of me sobbing in the airport.

I rented a car, not wanting to deal with having to get an Uber everywhere we went, so we pick it up first, talking about everything but the reason why I almost cried in the Phoenix International Airport.

My phone buzzes a couple of times with either Jesse or Jensen trying to call me, but I ignore it. It's stupid, and I can't avoid them forever, but I feel like I just need a couple more days before I talk to them.

Plus, there's a part of me that's still desperate to know what's going on with Tanner. And I know I won't be able to prevent myself from asking about him if I talk to them. It would probably push me off the deep end if I found out he was with that girl.

I had booked a boutique hotel, the Scott Resort, and Amberlie beamed as we stepped into the lobby that had been remade to be an Instagrammers' dream.

"Your two bedroom suite is ready for you. The pools are right through the lobby, and there's a cocktail hour tonight starting at seven, if you ladies are interested," the girl at the check-in desk says as she hands me a few bottles of water. I thank her before stepping away to walk to our room.

We get to our bedroom, and it's just as charming as the lobby. Bright gold details and mod pink decorate the space. There's a bar cart with ingredients to make specialty cocktails in the room, and the sliding glass doors open up to vibrantly blooming pink flowers. Even though my allergies are already acting up, it's one of the most charming hotels I've ever stayed at.

"Pool or talk?" Amberlie asks after we finish admiring the room.

"Let's go to the pool," I say, noting that my spray tan had already begun to fade.

After getting into our swimsuits, we walk out to one of the larger pools that has a sandy beach section. Everywhere you look, there are spots set up to take pictures.

The bloggers are out in full force, taking pictures of each other in their swimsuits at each one. One of the girls looks too closely at me, so I pull down my sun hat and turn towards Amberlie who is reading a magazine as she lounges in her chair.

"Only a few more months of school left," I comment. "What are your plans for the summer?"

"I think Teddy and I are going to take a long vacation. Maybe rent an Airbnb in California or something like that," she says excitedly. "He tries to save up all of his vacation time for during the summer when I'm off." I smile, and we begin to discuss some of the places I've been in California that she might like.

I watch as a group of girls set up on loungers across from us at the pool. They're giggling and laughing, snapping pictures and sipping on frozen cocktails. I wonder what it would be like to have been that carefree at any point in my life.

Shaking my head, I push the depressing thought out of my brain and soak up the sun, chatting about random things with Amberlie as we lounge. And I don't talk about the guys at all.

The next two days pass much the same way. Amberlie doesn't bring up the guys, and I know she's waiting for me to say something first. We go to the Fairmount Spa for one of the days and eat at Steak 44 for dinner, where I have the most amazing steak and lobster dish. It's a little surreal to me that I can actually afford to buy a meal like that by myself after a whole life of never having any of my own money.

I manage not to break down until the third day. We're sitting by the pool again when the radio station announces that Tanner Crosby from the Sound of Us has just released a solo single for the first time ever.

I drop the frozen margarita in my hand and only faintly register that its getting all over my beach bag.

You've seen the worst in me, and baby it's all true,
  But even the worst of me, only belongs to you.
  Hearts break every day, and mine's in pieces now too,
  Tell me all your secrets and I'll hide them away,
  Remember that night on the beach, and all the words you didn't say.

*My chance has come and gone, but I just want you to know,
That there's nothing I won't do to pay back the heart I owe.*

I'm crying on my chair as the song goes on. And I hear him. I hear his promises. And I hear how much he wants my forgiveness.

And I just know then, even if it doesn't make sense to anyone else. And even if it makes me look like a fool.

He loves me. He loved me on the beach that night when we were teenagers, and he's loved me every day since. He loves me in a way that doesn't go away… in a way that couldn't go away. And although I have a lot of questions about what happened with that girl…I'm still certain of one thing.

I love him too.

Somehow, more than I had yesterday or the day before that. Less than I would tomorrow for sure. In this moment, I realize that my love for Tanner had miraculously only grown during our time apart, and it was stronger than my doubt. If Tanner was lost, I would find him. If he was broken, I would fix him. I would always find a way to fix him, no matter what it took. There was no other alternative that was acceptable to me.

There never was with a love like ours.

Giving up just wasn't an option. Not anymore. Not without giving up on him. I saw Tanner for who he was. I loved him for the boy he was when I met him, the man he was, the man he wanted to be, and the man he would become.

I was all in. We would get through this. There was no other option.

I turn and see that Amberlie is patiently waiting and everything that has happened bursts out of me. I talk for hours, and she just listens. And when I'm done, I'm exhausted. But I feel free.

"Do you think I'm an idiot?" I finally ask.

And she smiles at me, her eyes a bit watery. "I think that the man who wrote that song is crazy in love with you. I know that the boy that man used to be sure was. And I think that maybe you always take a chance on a love like that. Even if it's a risk."

I hug her, because I need someone who believes in me right now. Who believes in us.

With that resolution in my mind, I get up and walk back to our room to get my phone. Picking it up, I hurriedly call him. I'm not surprised when he doesn't answer and his voicemail picks up.

"Hey," I begin, talking to the machine. "It's me. I mean you know it's me... What am I saying..." I take a deep breath.

"I've done a lot of thinking about what happened. About you and me. About us. And I've come to a realization. I don't believe you. I don't believe that you were with that girl. I don't believe that you would do that to me... do that to us. Even though I know the proof was right in front of me, Tanner...I know your heart. And I just don't believe your heart could do that to mine. I'm not sure why you're trying to push me away. And I'm trying to give you space, even though I'm not sure I should. But I just wanted you to know that I'll wait for you. I'll wait for you to get past whatever demons you're fighting right now because I know that I can't do this for you, I can't fight them for you. You have to do that by yourself, even as much as I want to do it for you."

"But you're in my veins, Tanner. You've lived inside of me since the moment I met you, I'm not gonna push you out now."

"So, what I'm trying to say to you is that I'll always love you. And I'll be here waiting for you when you decide to come back to me." I take a deep breath. "You're still my good thing."

I run through the story of us in my head. It seems like a lifetime. They introduced me to love, a concept so deep and expansive I couldn't imagine it. The pure, unadulterated emotion is an experience, a journey that comes along with loving them. Joy, awe, desire and passion, so much intense passion, is all part of the adventure. And so is the pain that sometimes comes with something like that.

My life before them was obscure. I'd never really started living until we met, I'd never really had the courage to. And I want the chance to have my happily-ever-after with them more than anything.

"I don't have a heart to give," Tanner once said to me. But clearly, it wasn't true. He didn't know it at the time, but his heart was full of love, and he gave it to me. They all did. And maybe I gave mine unwillingly at first, a protection against past hurts, but with time and patience, I became theirs. The truth of who we are together is woven indelibly between their hearts and mine. We belong to each other, mind, body and soul. There are no other people on this earth who understand me and know without a doubt exactly what I need to be whole. They offer me the perfect balance of self-discovery and forgiveness.

I need them.

I pick up the phone and call Jesse.

It's time for me to make things right.

.

24
NOW

TANNER

In rehab they taught you to be honest, or at least they tried their best to do that. The first couple of times I went, it hadn't stuck. But this time, it did.

"My name is Tanner, and I'm an addict," I announce to the room, hating the way the words taste as they come out of my mouth. They don't know I'm a big rockstar, they're all here because they're messed up just like me. We all just want to get better.

It's weird to tell my story to these people, the whole story, not just the pieces I told Ariana on the beach that night. In previous stays, I sat in my chair, kept my mouth shut, and did my time. I hadn't cared to get better. I was just trying to fulfill my label's mandate and get on with my life.

It took another week after Ariana left of abusing my body before I decided to come here.

I woke up on the floor, soaking wet from a bucket of water Jesse had poured all over me, bleeding because at some point in the night, my blacked-out self decided to try and end my pain with pieces of a broken beer bottle. I had been lucky that I didn't even need stitches, thanks to how drunk I was.

After making sure that I was alive, Jesse left, and I stayed on that floor for two days, sicker than I'd ever been, thanks to the withdrawal symptoms from quitting my steady supply of drugs cold turkey.

And that was the day that I decided that I either needed to die, or I needed to find a way to get better. Because this wasn't really living, whatever I was doing.

But even then, I checked myself out of rehab after a week and got drunk as soon as I saw a picture of Ari in the tabloids with Clark, the article speculating that they were now dating.

I immediately checked myself back in, still hungover. And this time, I stayed.

It had been three months now, and there were days where everything seemed insurmountable, like I was just a sum of all the mistakes that I had made.

But there were other days I kind of liked myself, and all I could hope was that Ari would like me again too.

"You have some guests," Dahlia, one of the nurses, tells me as she comes to the door of my room. I ignore the way her eyes devour me. I don't care about how any other woman looks at me, I just want Ariana to look at me.

I know who's waiting for me as I walk down the hall. Part of my therapy is righting the wrongs that I've done to people. And I'm sure there's a long list of them. But the fact that I'm an asshole means that I only really care about saying sorry to three of them. And two of them are here today.

Jesse and Jensen are my family. And I've hurt them over and over again. And yet, they've always stayed. It's more than I deserve.

I think I'm prepared for when I see them. I've been obsessing over what I was going to say for the last month. But my mind's blank when they actually come into view. And I'm suddenly afraid this is where they tell me that they're done with me, because who would want to put up with someone like me after so long?

But Jesse stands when he sees me, a big grin on his face as he stalks across the room and pulls me into a back-thumping hug. "It's good to see you, Tan," he says, and as he pulls away, his eyes look suspiciously wet.

Jensen's hanging back, his hands in his pockets. I've said some of the worst things to him, and I've rarely said sorry. That he's here at all is a surprise.

"Hey," I say, awkwardly waving my hand. Which makes Jensen's mouth twitch, because I'm rarely awkward.

"Let's go into one of the visitor rooms so we don't have everyone watching us," Jesse says, gesturing behind us at the room that's starting to fill up as news that the Sound of Us is here.

Separately we can-for the most part-go unnoticed as long as we aren't walking around LA, but all together, we're kind of hard to miss.

We walk into the small room. It's just a table and a few chairs with a small window on one wall. The silence is deafening, and I know that I need to say something, but after all my planning, I'm not sure now that I'll have anything that's adequate for the things I've done.

"I'm sorry," slips out of my mouth and Jesse smiles patiently. Jensen looks non-plussed though.

"You know, she barely talked to us for months," he says, looking away from me to out of the window. "She texted us, maybe a phone call here and there, but other than that, it was radio silence. I had to get my updates through Clark."

"But she's talking to you now?" I ask. I didn't expect to be able to get to talk about Ariana right away, if at all. And now that he's opened the gates, I'm desperate.

"She called us a few weeks back. And she sounded different. More at peace," Jensen explains, still not looking at me.

"Have you seen her? How's her tour going?" The words

come rushing out, and this isn't how I wanted the conversation to go but I can't stop.

"Yeah, we've seen her. She's perfect. Sad, but perfect," says Jesse quietly, his eyes out of focus as if he's seeing her in his mind right now. "She misses you."

Jensen stands up and walks to the window abruptly. "I just want you to know that if she hadn't come back to us, I would have never forgiven you," he announces.

"I know. I would have deserved that," I respond to him.

He looks at me surprised.

I shrug my shoulders. "Honestly, the fact that you guys are here is more than I deserve. I've been messed up for a long time. And I just wanted to tell you a little bit about why."

Jesse straightens in his seat, and after a long minute, Jensen comes back to the table and sits down.

And then I proceed to tell my brothers -for the first time- what was going on when we were growing up, and what's been in my head since.

Jesse looks sick after I've finished, and Jensen looks guilt-ridden.

"Why the fuck didn't you tell us?" he finally says.

"You were already going through enough, and Jesse had his hands full trying to take care of our asses. It's stupid, but I just didn't feel like I could say anything. The only person who knew some of it was Ari, and I made her promise to never say anything."

They don't look surprised that Ari knew. We've all given her the darkest parts of us from the beginning.

"So those scars were from your dad?" asks Jesse, hoarsely.

I nod, and he beats on the table with a fist. "Fuck. I feel like an idiot."

"No, you just fell for the narrative that I gave you guys. Which is what I wanted then. But I've come to learn the hard way how bad secrets are for me. And I'm done with them." My voice gets choked up. "And I just want you to know that

I'm sorry for being such a stupid fuck all these years. And never getting help. And I just want you to know that I didn't sleep with that girl. I didn't even touch her. I couldn't."

Jesse nods knowingly. "I didn't think you had."

Jensen's head is lowered, and his shoulders are tense. When they start to shake, I realize that he's crying. Jensen Reid is crying.

And then we're all kind of crying, and it's actually a little bit embarrassing and wonderful all at the same time.

There's a knock on the door, and of course, Dahlia is on the other side. "Your hour is up," she says, and I nod, trying to hide the fact that I've been crying. Technically, I could just ask them to extend the hour visitation rule for me, but I'm determined to do everything right this stay, which means following all the stupid rules to the letter.

We all stand up and get ahold of ourselves before walking out.

And it's amazing how much better I feel, and how much better they look. My problems have been a burden on all of us for as long as I can remember, and I know that we're all feeling hopeful that this can be the turning point.

But something tells me that even if I ever fell again, my brothers would still be by my side.

When they're about to leave, Jensen suddenly turns around and looks at me. "Check your voicemail," he says, and I look at him confused.

"Just do it, man."

And I nod, all of a sudden itching to go to the office and get my phone that I've been living without since I got here.

I watch as they disappear from sight before I head to the office. "Hey, can I have my phone for a minute?" I charmingly ask the front desk woman, Lucille I think is her name.

"You know you only get five minutes with it," she says, trying to sound hard, but she's blushing. I nod as I take it from her and power it on. I haven't checked it out once since I got here.

The phone immediately alerts me that I have about 3000 new texts and missed calls, but I head to my voicemail, knowing immediately what Jensen wanted me to look for.

My heart skips a beat as I see the one message from Ariana dated a few months back. My hand is shaking as I press on the message and then put it up to my ear.

Her voice washes over me, and it feels like I'm having a fucking heart attack as she speaks.

"But you're in my veins, Tanner. You've lived inside of me since the moment I met you, I'm not gonna push you out now.

So, what I'm trying to say to you is that I'll always love you. And I'll be here waiting for you when you decide to come back to me. You're still my good thing."

And I smile as I press on the message to listen again. Because somehow, I know everything is going to be okay.

I'm going to give Ariana her happily-ever-after, even if it's the last thing I do.

25
NOW

ARIANA

It's the last night of my tour. Clark's already talking about wanting me to go on a bigger one in a few months, but I can't think ahead that far, not with everything that's going on. Jesse and Jensen have both flown in, and so have Amberlie and her husband. Four of my favorite people in the world are laughing and joking with each other as I look over the set list one more time.

It was my biggest show by far, opening for Tyler Rowe, a pop singer that was almost as big as the Sound of Us. Apparently, he actually opened up for them at one point and was pretty good friends with the band, so he had been hanging around for most of the day as well. I laughed to myself thinking about how Tyler tried flirting with Amberlie at first and how fast Teddy swooped in.

It made my heart happy to see my friends so happy. Or at least, as happy as my heart could feel with the empty hole that was Tanner.

He never answered my voicemail. It had been three months, and I wondered if I would ever stop obsessing about how he was doing. All my talk about finding myself, becoming my own person... I had come to a realization over the last three months that I wasn't me without Jesse, Tanner, and Jensen, all of them.

And it was the same for them.

Somehow along the way, we became permanently connected. We were written in each other's hearts, in our very DNA. And I didn't know if there was enough time in the world to change me back if Tanner never returned.

"I'm starting to get jealous about how much time you spend pining over Tanner," a voice whispers in my ear. The velvet quality of Jensen's voice washes over me, and I savor his warmth as he pulls me into him. "That asshole's fucking lucky to have you," he says, but there's no real heat in his voice. I know Jensen misses Tanner and is worried about him almost as much as I am.

Jesse joins us a minute later.

"You totally did that on purpose," he scoffs at Jensen with a disgusted look on his face.

I quirk an eyebrow at Jensen who looks wickedly delighted by Jesse's reaction.

"How else was I going to get a second with our girl?" he says with a grin.

I see Jesse's mouth twitch like he wants to smile, but he's trying to hold it back.

"What did he do?" I say with a laugh, still surprised that I'm able to laugh again.

"One of Tyler's groupies wasn't getting the message that Jensen was sending that she needed to back off. So asshole over here sicced her on me so he could get some alone time with you."

I can't help but giggle, but at the same time, think how surreal this easiness between the three of us is. I wasn't worried about other women, I wasn't worried about them leaving me. It was like our pieces finally clicked into place.

I guess the time apart helped with that, although if I was honest, there hadn't been much of that since I called them from Scottsdale. Between them flying out to see me after every show, and vice versa, there had only been a few nights that we've spent apart. And I was definitely all right with that, even though Clark continued to encourage me to be more independent.

The first opening act finishes up, signaling that it's almost my turn. There were at least 30,000 people in the arena, and my stomach was fluttering crazily at the thought. We just released my third single, another one that I had written, and it took off like the others, even surpassing the first two, somehow.

I cried last night when Clark called and told me to check the charts, and I saw that somehow "Memories of Us" made it to number one on Billboard making me the first woman in pop history to have three #1s in my debut album. The only thing missing in that perfect moment was Tanner, and I hoped that somehow, he had access to the radio and would somehow stumble upon the song.

I lean into Jensen to give him a kiss and see that he looks concerned as he stares out into the crowd. He and Jesse stopped giving me a hard time about safety, but the threat was always there that Gentry was out there. There had been no surprise packages from him over the last month, and the silence was scarier than his gifts were.

I lost confidence that he was going to be found and was trying to come to terms with the fact that he might always be haunting me, a mistake that shouldn't have been permanent, but would be.

Jensen wipes the worried look from his face when he sees me looking and gives me a kiss that heats me up in all the right places. Jensen would be coming out to sing Tanner's part of our song a little later.

Jesse grabs me away from Jensen when the kiss goes on

for too long, and I laugh at his mock jealousy. He starts kissing down the side of my neck, sending shivers catapulting across my body.

"I can't wait for some alone time with you," he growls, before kissing the hell out of me too.

"You're on," the disgruntled stage manager barks at me while Jesse continues to maul my face. I pull away, unable to keep the smile off my face.

"Break a leg, pretty girl," Jesse says, and I lose my breath for a second at the love I can see in his eyes, in both of their eyes.

No matter what happened, I was a lucky girl.

Taking a deep breath, I walk out on stage, the nervous energy driving my adrenaline higher.

I raise my hand and wave to the crowd before immediately jumping into the first song. It's the song that I released as my second single, and even though the song reached #1 on the charts, the fact that this crowd of 30,000 is actually singing my words back to me was unbelievable. No longer were people not showing up for the opening act when I was performing. The arena was almost as full as it would be when Tyler stepped on stage.

I had to actively work to make sure that the emotion I was feeling didn't show in my voice. But that girl singing with me at that first performance meant just as much to me as the arena full of people singing back to me did now.

Now I understood how artists could perform for a year singing the same album, and never get tired of it. There was nothing like this.

The song ends, and right before I'm about to open my mouth to address the crowd, a feeling passes over me. A feeling that someone is watching me. My heart starts pounding faster as I scan the crowd. Not recognizing anyone in the immediate rows in front of me, I try to block out the feeling.

"How are we today, Dallas?" I belt out, a big smile lighting up my face as the crowd roars back at me. "My name is Ariana Kent, and if you haven't heard of me, that's all right. I'm hoping we get to be good friends by the end of the night. It's still hard for me to believe that I'm getting to perform in front of you tonight and opening for Tyler Rowe, one of my favorite artists on the planet." The crowd screams even louder at mention of Tyler's name.

"What about the Sound of Us boys?" someone a few rows in front of me calls out, and I freeze, because I recognize that voice. I would recognize that voice anywhere.

It takes me a second, but I finally find him. Tanner Crosby is standing in the fourth row, center stage, a baseball cap pulled down low over his face, but there's no way I wouldn't recognize those silver eyes as they pierce right through me.

I purse my lips, trying not to cry. "Let's get started then," I announce to the crowd, ripping my eyes away from Tanner. He looks good, better than good. He looks healthy. Gone are the sunken cheeks and the shadowed eyes. He looks better than I've ever seen him, like all the things that had been haunting him on the inside had finally been fixed.

I don't know how I get through the next song, because my eyes keep going back to him. He's staring at me like I'm the only person in the world that exists. And when he mouths to me that he loves me, I almost have to stop singing altogether.

Why was he doing this? Why is he here after months of nothing? Had he listened to my voicemail? Had he waited for me, just like I had waited for him?

I'm distracted in the next song as well, and when I glance over to Jensen and Jesse, I can tell that they've noticed.

"What's going on?" Jensen mouths, and I widen my eyes, hoping that he can somehow read what I'm thinking. It takes him a moment, but I can see when he gets it, because he nearly jumps out of the skin. "Tanner," he mouths, and I give him a small nod. He blanches and quickly tells Jesse. I can see that it's taking everything in them not to take a few steps farther out onto the stage so they can see him too.

But that would definitely ruin my set, if I wasn't already ruining it by how distracted I am.

My next song is actually fitting for the situation. I wrote it when I had lost them the first time. And it was filled with all the tragedy of youth and lost love. It matched my current situation with Tanner perfectly as well.

I can tell that he identified with the emotion and the song as I'm singing it, because his silver eyes get soft, the way they did when he was truly sad. He looks hopeless after I finish singing, and even though it hadn't been my intention, Tanner is probably thinking the worst about us.

And maybe I'm naïve, but I'm still so hopeful that everything can be explained after the last few months. I want to make him feel better, I want him to know that I still believe in him, believe in us. The next song on my set is supposed to be a cover of Lady Antebellum that I was going to perform on the piano. But I decide to change it to one that always reminds me of Tanner instead. The stage crew quickly rolls out the piano, and I sit down at it.

"I've found that sometimes, maybe most of the time, music is able to more accurately say what I'm feeling than anything else. Some of you might recognize this next one. It's called 'Yours', originally performed by Ella Henderson," I tell the crowd, immediately eliciting more cheers.

Taking a deep breath, I begin to play.

I wear your winter coat...

The song is a perfect message for my lover. And I feel its words right down to my soul. When I look up, Tanner's eyes have that soft look about them still, but this time, I know it's because of happiness.

And I know every day you say it
  But I just want you to be sure
  That I'm yours...

I keep my head bowed when I finish as I try to get ahold of myself. The crowd is screaming so loud right now, it's like they know why I picked this song.

I try to get my act together, performing a few originals and a few more covers, and then it's time for Jensen to come perform with me.

Just like always, it's magic singing with him. Everything else, even Tanner's presence, is forgotten as we stare at each other and pour out the words that we wrote together. The crowd's screams are deafening, especially when Jensen pulls me into a kiss after we're done that's too hot for public consumption.

I'm sure I have a goofy smile as he leaves the stage.

I'm just about to perform my last song, when I see him. It's not Tanner this time, but a haggard looking Gentry. He's making his way through the crowd until he's standing in the third row right in front of me.

I'm frozen in place. The look in his eyes is crazed, and all I can think in that moment is that I'm about to die, and there's still so much life I want to live.

People begin screaming around him as he pulls a gun out from under his plaid flannel and points it at me. His hands are shaking, but he looks determined.

Suddenly Tanner is tackling him, and they're wrestling each other for the gun.

I scream as Gentry knocks Tanner in the side of the head

with the gun. Jesse and Jensen come bursting out onto the stage, running towards me, but I'm still frozen in place watching the scene in front of me play out.

Tanner's on his knees, struggling to get his wits together after being knocked in the head. Gentry begins to stalk towards me again and it's mass chaos as people trample over one another trying to get away from the madman with a gun.

I finally begin to back away, not willing to turn around and run and not be able to see it when he shoots. Gentry raises the gun again and I see his finger twitch on the trigger, and then Tanner is once again on him. They fall to the ground this time, struggling with the gun.

Boom, the shots ring out through the stadium, and I sink to my knees as I see Tanner's still form on top of Gentry.

"NOOOO," I scream, the sound echoing through the stadium since I'm wearing a mike.

Jesse reaches me and throws himself in front of me while Jensen launches himself into the crowd, trying to get to Tanner.

Even though it's stupid and there's nothing I can do, I try to buck Jesse off of me so that I can get to Tanner too. The whole stadium screaming is a million times worse than what it sounded like last time. I was in hell, and I knew that if I lived past this moment, sounds of today would haunt me for the rest of my life.

Jesse is looking towards Tanner, an ugly, frightened look on his face that I never want to see again. I look away from him and see that Jensen has reached Tanner and Gentry.

Gentry landed on top of Tanner in the scuffle, and I can see crimson blood spreading out on the concrete floor around them now that the crowd has run away. Jensen rips Gentry off of Tanner, and I realize that Gentry isn't moving either, not even when his head slams against the concrete floor as he's flipped onto his back.

And then Tanner, my beautiful sad boy, is sitting up, a little unsteadily...but he's standing up.

Choking sobs fall from my mouth, this time sobs of relief. He's covered in blood, but there aren't any visible holes in his shirt, and when I look at Gentry, I can see a gaping hole where his heart should have been. Tanner staggers for a second before shaking his head like he's trying to get his head straight, and Jensen is patting him all over checking for injuries. Tanner shakes his head again, hopefully saying this time that he isn't injured. Jensen lets out a choked sob and throws his arms around Tanner.

Jesse finally moves off me, staying close though and gripping my hand tight, as if he's prepared to jump in front of me again at any sign of danger. After I get up, I stand there, a little shakily myself from the adrenaline, watching Tanner and Jensen. It's like the whole world shrinks at that moment, and it's just the four of us.

Tanner finally settles those haunting silver eyes on me, and I'm off the stage in a flash this time, dragging Jesse behind me. When I get to Tanner and Jensen, I throw one arm around both of them, burying my face in Tanner's neck while still holding tightly to Jesse.

As we stand there, wrapped in each other's arms, I'm only faintly aware of the SWAT team running around the area. Someone's checking Gentry's pulse, but I know that he's dead.

It's like my body can sense that he's taken his final breath, and I'm finally free.

I thought over these last couple of months, that something was wrong with our love, that it was a shade of wrong that perhaps couldn't be overcome.

But now, I can see our love for what it is, beautifully broken, just like the four of us.

26
NOW

TANNER

After we'd all talked to the authorities, and I'd been taken to the hospital for precautionary measures, and she'd made sure I was fine, she'd told Jesse and Jensen she needed to get away for a day and she left.

I find her at the beach house she bought, just an hour outside of LA. It was the first thing she'd gotten with her paycheck apparently.

And it's perfect.

It's all white and modern looking with windows everywhere. I knew that Ariana always liked big windows after growing up in a trailer that didn't have any. I walk around the side of the house and see that it sits on a pristine strip of private beach, and it immediately becomes my new favorite place. Maybe because it reminds me of the beach house we used to go to.

I knock on the back door, but she doesn't answer. I try to open the door next. It's unlocked, which shows how at ease Ariana is feeling now that Gentry is gone.

I open the door slowly and enter the house, my movements making quiet creaks of protest from the home. Everything is silent and still. I peek into a modern, gourmet kitchen on my left and a dining room on my right before ascending the steps.

I'm nervous. I brush my sweaty hands down the sides of my pants. My heart beats so loud in my chest, so solidly, as if making me aware of its frantic state is necessary. I reach the top step, and call out her name into the dark.

There's an open doorway directly across from the staircase, and I know she's in there. I swear I can hear her heartbeat. It was hers, the rhythm as familiar as my own.

A moment later I hear her voice. "Tanner." I'm nearly brought to my knees but I move, approaching the door slowly, the sound of her heartbeat ringing in my ears, her heavy breaths coming closer. And then she stands there, silhouetted in the doorway, looking like she expected me to come.

"Tanner," she says, this time with relief. I can't wait a moment longer. I step into the doorway and as I reach my arms for her, she jumps, right into my arms, right where I need her to be always.

I hold her tightly, afraid to let her go and lose her again. My nose burrows in her hair and I breathe in her sweet scent and exhale a breath I didn't know I was holding.

"Ari," I murmur into her hair, feeling my heart settle its rhythm, my chest loosen and allow me to breathe more normally.

She pulls back, and her hands find my face. Her eyes are glistening. She's beautiful, she's always been beautiful, but seeing the emotion in her eyes makes my own tighten with the surge of relief I feel that we're reunited.

Her fingers roam my face, touching my features, as if the moment is a dream. And that's what it feels like. Holding her, seeing her, it's the sweetest dream.

My lips descend quickly, impatient for that connection to

her. Her hands grip my hair, she moans a small sound that reverberates through her mouth into mine, and I fall in love with this woman all over again.

I need Ariana like I need breath. Possibly more.

She pulls back, and this time her cheeks are wet, and there's a shaky smile on her lips.

"You're here." I touch a finger to her lips and rub reassuringly. "I missed you, Princess," I say, even though the words fall painfully short of the full depth of emotions I've had during this time apart.

Her head falls back, and she lets out a laugh, the sound I didn't know I needed to hear so desperately. Fuck, she's the most incredibly stunning creature on earth.

And she's still mine. And she still loves me.

She lets her head fall to rest on my shoulder, her hands finding my waist and gripping me tightly. "Understatement of the year, I think, Tanner." I close my eyes. Hearing her say my name, hearing the word roll off her lips, this was what I'd longed for. I wrap my arms around her tightly and kiss her hair.

I know I won't let go of her anytime soon.

I hold her in the doorway, catching up on the months I missed with her.

She spins around and grabs my hand, pulling me into the room with her. The moment we are inside the room, she shuts the door and walks backwards from me. My eyes stay locked on hers, and I'm only faintly aware of the floor to ceiling windows that take up the whole far wall of the room that must be her bedroom.

I watch her, mesmerized, as she keeps her eyes on me. She pulls the t-shirt she's wearing up and over her head before she tosses it at me, biting on her lip. I hadn't seen this playful side of her in a long time. I'd missed her, desperately.

But I'm not feeling playful. The swelling in my chest, knowing this wasn't one of my many dreams, was overpowering me and my movements. I hold the shirt in my hands, and keeping my eyes trained on hers, I bring it up to my face and inhale.

I watch her face change. The playful glint leaves her eyes. In its place is heady desire. I feel my whole body change, shift into a familiar place. Don't get me wrong. It wasn't that I didn't love seeing her playful side. But my heart is burning in my chest, and I had seriously intense feelings for her, feelings that stole my air and changed the rhythm of my heartbeat.

In Ariana, I found more than love, more than hope and peace.

I found my home.

I walk slowly to her, watching the movement of her throat as she swallows. My eyes move to meet hers the moment my hands touch her skin. Each time I touch her, my fingers come alive, as if she's the most beautiful instrument my hands would ever touch. I press my lips to her forehead, feel the heat of her breath on my neck. My eyes close, and I savor this moment, savor being home again. My fingers slide from her arms up and over her shoulders, touching her neck. My thumbs trace her jaw line, meeting at the center of her chin. My thumbs tremble when I watch her lips part.

Every single part of her was made perfectly for me.

I brush a thumb over her lips and look into her eyes again. They're clouded over with lust. Seeing that lights a match in my veins. My arms move to encircle her as my mouth touches hers. I capture the breath she's about to take and sink in, lips and tongues and nibbles from teeth.

"Tanner," she moans against my mouth.

I lift her up, relishing in the feel of her weight in my arms. I crush her body to mine, unwinding her hair from its messy bun, and dive my fingers into the strands. I turn around and sit on the edge of her massive bed, so she's in my lap, kissing me as passionately as I was kissing her. I pull back to catch my breath, our noses pressed against each other. I fill my lungs as I look at her.

"You are every dream I've ever had," I say, my voice sounding foreign even to me. I cup her cheek with one hand while she looks at me, eyes open and unguarded. "I don't think you'll ever understand how much I need you."

She swallows hard, sucking in air. "Tanner," she says softly, and the words comes out pained and lonely, exactly how I've felt without her in my life.

I whisper a kiss down the side of her face.

"Say you still love me," I murmur as I continue to move across her skin.

There's a pause before she answers.

"Always," and a small smile appears on her lips.

I return her smile, feeling an ache blooming in my chest at having her here, in my arms again. I want to bury myself in her smiles, in the way she looks at me. On impulse, I pull her to me again, hugged her tightly. I breath in her scent again and send up a silent thank you to the powers that be.

"Tanner," she says against my neck.

"Hmm?" I murmur against her hair.

"I really want to make out. Now."

I pull back abruptly and seal my lips to hers. I feel her purr in the back of her throat. She pushes me so I'm laying on my back, with her on top of me, her hair a curtain around us. Bliss. That's what it is. I run my hands up her back, along the line of her spine until I touch her bra. She pulls back as if expecting me to unsnap it, but instead, my fingers follow along to the front of the bra, over the cups, over her curves. I hear her suck in a breath, and a second later, her delicate hands are on my shoulders, pulling me up before pulling my shirt up over my head. When my shirt was gone, she runs her hands down my chest, over my stomach. My muscles clench involuntarily, and I move away from her, remembering we still have things we need to talk about. She keeps running her hands all over me though, and I'm having trouble thinking.

"Wait, Ari," I tell her. "We need to talk."

"Shhh. I know that you didn't have anything to do with that girl," she says as she begins to lay kisses across my chest.

"You do?" I ask, my heart feeling like its going to explode, because somehow, she believes in me.

"Yes...now kiss me," she commands.

I flip us so she's on her back, looking up at me with the light from the windows lighting up half of her face. Her lips are swollen and parted, her eyes heavy-lidded. It spurs impatience in me, so I grab the hem of her shorts and yank, pulling them down. I stand up to remove them and remove my jeans.

I can't keep my eyes off of her. She stares at me, into me, from her position on the bed. My blood pounds in my veins.

"You're everything to me," I tell her.

She bites her lip, and the corners of her eyes crinkle. "Show me," she whispers.

I step between her legs and run my hands up her calves, over her thighs, squeezing every few inches. I feel her skin tremble beneath my hands and I smile calmly, patiently, at her. Her eyes are burning with lust, their golden depths the darkest shade I'd seen them.

When I reach her underwear, I run a finger just under the seam, back and forth along her stomach. Gently, I grab the sides and pull them slowly down her legs.

"Tanner," she pleads this time, impatience clear in her voice.

But I still move slowly, unwilling to rush this. When I've removed her underwear, I take her hand and pull so she's standing with me. I push a soft kiss to her lips before turning her around, her back to my front. I move her hair to rest over one shoulder. I rub a thumb over the tattoo on her side and kiss a line over the gorgeous curve that exists between her neck and her shoulder.

My hands move to the middle of her back, and unsnap the bra while my lips press kisses across her exposed shoulder.

"I'll never have enough time," I whisper against her skin. "Eternity won't be long enough to love you."

I put my lips to her ear, nibbling on her lobe.

"But I can try," I breath as I push the straps off her shoulders. My hands move around to her front, cupping her breasts. Her head falls back onto my shoulder, and I kiss the side of her neck, while I squeeze her gently. "You're flawless, Princess."

"I think you're trying to make love to me with your words, Tanner," she says, her eyes closed, her chest heaving with exertion.

I turn her around so she's facing me again and push the hair from her face.

"Every single part of me wants that. I want to fill your thoughts, so that there isn't room for anything else but us." I push her gently, so she's naked, on her back on the bed. "You've filled my thoughts since day one." I climb over her. She looks up at me, her eyes full of emotion. She lifts a hand to cup my face.

"You do, Tanner," she whispers earnestly. I lean down and kiss her, feeling my heartbeat settle in my chest. And then my body joins with hers again and again, in a dance that belongs only to us, with the music only we can hear. And when we both reach our release, I swear I'll never be happier than this moment.

Later, Ariana lays on my chest, drawing circles with her finger on my skin. "Tell me about the last few months," she orders, sleepily. I run my fingers through her hair as we go over all my therapy, all the realizations I came to.

She's asleep before I can tell her about the months of agony, of the dreams and the nightmares, the way I yearned desperately for this, for her breath on my skin, her body in my arms, her heartbeat in my ear.

But it doesn't matter that she's fallen asleep. Because every single second of her sleeping on my chest is worth all the months of missing her, missing this.

I wake her later, unable to keep myself away from her.

"I will love you through this life and into the next. Let me show you," I whisper to her.

And there's nothing gentle about our joining. Our time apart has been a lesson of negligence. We'd both gotten lost in the shit this life had thrown our way, drifting from what we needed the most. This. Us. Individually we're broken in pieces, but together, somehow, we're fixed, and I'm irrevocably in love with her the way I'd always dreamed of being.

Ariana Kent will forever be my good thing.

27
3 MONTHS LATER

ARIANA

"Justin Timberlake just said hello to me," I squeal to no one in particular.

Jensen growls and nips at my lips.

"You do know that each of us has been voted People's Sexist Man Alive for the past three years straight, right?" remarks Jesse amusedly, raising his eyebrow at my fan girl moment.

"Yes, but I didn't have posters of you on my walls growing up, did I?" I tease.

And this time, Jesse growls. I lean into him and grab his hand, fluttering my eyelashes ridiculously. "Is someone jealous of Justin?" I murmur with a wink.

He presses a scorching kiss against my lips, and I feel so happy that it seems unreal.

We're walking the red carpet. At the Grammy's.

And I can't believe that this is somehow my life.

I've been nominated for three awards tonight. New Artist of the Year, Record of the Year, and Album of the Year. And I'll be performing twice tonight. Once with Tanner of our single, and another by myself.

Tanner's also up for song of the year for the solo song he put out while we were apart, something that the guys razz him mercilessly about. Sound of Us isn't up for any of awards tonight, as their last album didn't release in time to be eligible for this year's ceremony. But they've already broken several records with the Grammy's they've already won, so I don't feel too bad for them that they will be going home empty-handed tonight.

Things have been good, the kind of good where you hold your breath, because you're sure that it can't last forever. Dr. Mayfield tells me that this is normal after everything that's happened, and that it will just take time for me to trust that this is my life now.

Tanner hasn't relapsed once. He has a sponsor, and he goes to meetings every week, no matter where we are. And he's so happy and healthy that it feels like I'm meeting Tanner for the first time.

I look down at the sparkling set of three diamond bands on my left hand, and I lose my breath for a second, thinking of last week when I got them.

I walk into the living room, and I gasp. There are white candles burning throughout the room, hundreds of them.

Did I miss an anniversary, I wonder?

Just then, Jensen walks in, dressed in jeans and a simple tee shirt, his feet bare. He walks over to me, the love he feels for me shining out from his very soul.

Music starts just then, a Halsey song that I've always loved.

He grabs my hand and pulls me to him, and we start dancing, the flames from the candles flickering and casting a romantic glow as we move. He starts to sing in my ear.

You stopped me in my tracks and put me right in my place

Used to think that loving meant a painful chase
But you're right here now and I think you'll stay

The lyrics float over me, and I know this song was meant for me. Because after everything I've been through, I've finally found my safe place. A place that I can fall. A place that I can stay.

Jensen spins me playfully, and I find myself in Jesse's arms, and he smiles as he whispers that he loves me. We continue to dance and I bury my face in the crook of Jesse's neck. This boy who has always been there for me, who believed in us from the very beginning.

I'm spun again, this time finding myself in Tanner's arms. Beautiful stranger indeed, I think, since this Tanner is alive and whole.

The music changes to Ben Fold's "The Luckiest", and tears are streaming down my face now because I think I know what's coming, and I can't believe it. We sway as Tanner sings to me about loving me in a way that surpasses his ability to say.

When the music finally stops, he pulls away. And I turn around and see that the three of them are all on one knee, boxes outstretched in each of their hands.

"Ariana Kent, will you marry me?" they each ask, one after another. And all I can do is nod as they get up and slip diamond bands on my left finger, one on top of the other.

And I know in this moment, it's me that is the luckiest.

We're in our seats, and I'm tapping my heeled foot nervously because Album of the Year is the next award. Jesse squeezes my hand reassuringly, wanting me to win just as much I want to win.

We've decided that I'll legally marry Jesse. It just makes sense, because out of the three of them, Jesse has always been my rock. He's never faltered in his belief in us. He's never faltered in his love for me.

And then the presenters are calling my name.

And the guys are all hugging me and pushing me forward so I can walk onto the stage.

And I'm standing there, in front of the whole industry, barely able to talk because of this moment.

And my heart is exploding with joy.

And I realize that the broken girl from the trailer park, the one who had no hope, no dreams, no future...she finally found her happily-ever-after, after all.

EPILOGUE
5 YEARS LATER

"Mommy, watch me," Danny cries as he races as fast as his chubby little legs can manage. I clap loudly for him.

That boy with silver eyes, the boy with wild sunshine inside of him, and the boy that writes words that make me cry...they're all mine. As I watch them race around, chasing the little girl and little boy that we've created together, a million memories race through my mind like a brilliant tapestry of our lives.

I thought I loved them when we met, I thought that I loved them when I found them once again, but this right here...I never comprehended I would love them like this, or that they would love me like this in return.

I know when we're old and grey, it will be hard to remember every minute of the life that we've worked so hard to build together. But sitting here on this porch, watching them as the sun fades in the distance and the fireflies spark to life, I know that I won't ever forget right now.

I'll always remember us this way.

The End

Join my newsletter for a bonus scene from The Sound of Us series.

ACKNOWLEDGMENTS

Well, somehow we're here…at the end.

And it's a little bit hard for me to be here because I've never ended a series before, and I'm pretty sure that Ari and her boys took a piece of me with them this book.

I have never cried more while writing a book. But I promised you a happy ending, and even though it hurt…we got there.

And in my head, Ari and her boys are so happy, forever and ever in fact.

I've always been influenced by music in my writing, but never like I was in this book. I would literally hear a song, and an entire chapter would change so that I could write what I felt when listening to that song. Big shout out to Beautiful Stranger by Halsey by the way, because that proposal scene definitely came from that song.

Other parts of this book will always be special to me as well. I put little stories from my own life into my stories and I found myself doing that more than ever in this one. An example of this is when Tanner is talking about getting swept out to sea and watching as the world above him got smaller and smaller. That happened to me when I was five and living in Hawaii.

Before we go, and we must…which is a hard pill to swallow. I just wanted to give out some thank you's.

First off, my beta for this book, Caitlin…you are spectacular. And now you are a doctor apparently because Dr. Madison obviously came from your name.

Meghan Daigle, thanks for working so freaking hard on this book with me even when I needed to send it to you chapter by chapter, and even when I needed it done right at the deadline.

Mila and Rebecca, thanks for being my girls…and always supporting me when I feel like I can't write another word. Or when I'm crying because my characters make me so sad.

Thanks to my family, because this takes a lot of sacrifice on their part to see me walking around with stories in my head and dreams in my eyes as my characters call out to me at random hours of the day.

And last…thanks to you. Because I feel a little bit like Ari did that you guys actually read my work. Every time I get a message or a question about my books…I just think, is this real life?

Thanks for letting me do something that I love so much.

I'll always remember us this way.

Broken
Hearts
Academy
Book 1

HEARTBREAK PRINCE

INTERNATIONAL BESTSELLING AUTHOR
C.R. JANE

Heartbreak Prince by C. R. Jane

Copyright © 2020 by C. R. Jane

All rights reserved.

No portion of this book may be reproduced in any form or by any electronic or mechanical means, including information storage and retrieval systems, without written permission from the author, except for the use of brief quotations in a book review, and except as permitted by U.S. copyright law.

For permissions contact:

crjaneauthor@gmail.com

This book is a work of fiction. Names, characters, businesses, places, events, locales, and incidents are either the products of the author's imagination or used in a fictitious manner. Any resemblance to actual persons, living or dead, or actual events is purely coincidental.

HEARTBREAK PRINCE

Soulmates. I believe in them. I was lucky enough to have two of them at one point.

The only problem. *My soulmates happened to be twin brothers.*

Caiden was the light to Jackson's dark. And after all that I had been through, the light was what I thought I needed.

When I chose Caiden, I lost Jackson.

Feeling like half a person after Jackson left, I barely survived when tragedy struck and I lost Caiden too.

It took me years to admit to myself that I had chosen wrong from the beginning. I'm ready to admit it to Jackson… only problem, he hates me.

I'm ready to fight for my happily ever after.

But there's a reason they call him the Heartbreak Prince.

HEARTBREAK PRINCE SOUNDTRACK

Why Are You Here
(Machine Gun Kelly)

Chasing Cars
(Snow Patrol)

Yours
(No Love For The Middle Child)

Breathe (2 AM)
(Anna Nalick)

Past Life
(Trevor Daniel)

One Thing Right
(Marshmello & Kane Brown)

Happier
(Marshmello & Bastille)

Kiss Me
(Sixpence None The Richer)

Delicate
(Taylor Swift)

Never Be The Same
(Camilla Cabello)

Without You
(Ingrid Michaelson)

Portions for Foxes
(Rilo Kiley)

I lost my virginity to an angel...but my first and last kiss was with the devil.
And that's everything you need to know about me.

Sometimes when it's really dark outside, and I feel particularly alone. I allow myself to remember us. It doesn't happen often, because I wouldn't be able to function otherwise, but I just wanted you to know that everything about us is like perfect Technicolor in my memory.

CHAPTER 1

THEN

I was eight when we met. *Do you remember that?* I was in third grade. I was small for my age, and all the other kids picked on me. They had plenty of things to go after—who my father was, my slight lisp, how my clothes were all too baggy, and how I didn't have a running washing machine at my house, and so oftentimes my clothes weren't quite as clean as they should have been...because washing clothes in the sink could only go so far. All were fair game. My classmates had made my life a living hell all through elementary school. And I expected it to continue...until the two of you started school.

You started a new school that year. You and your brother had just moved into town. You were only a few months older than me, but you weren't scared of anything. And when you saw me on the playground, and you saw how some of the kids had picked up rocks from the ground and were going to throw them at me, you marched right in. And while Caiden was yelling at them to stop, you were the one who actually tackled Marshall, the biggest kid, who had been particularly awful to me for years. And you didn't even know me.

And when you got up after punching him several times,

your lip was bleeding, but you gave me the biggest smile and told me it was all going to be okay.

Do you remember that?

Neither of us noticed the fact that Caiden was also looking at me.

Wasn't it funny how a story like ours could happen like that, even at that young of an age?

We were best friends after you and Caiden defended me that day. Maybe the two of you were more than best friends to me, maybe you were my saviors. Because after years of living in hell, you made sure that school became my safe place.

Remember how Caiden always used to bring extra for lunch, and pretend that he wasn't hungry, but he would actually give it to me? I was in the free lunch program, but both of you thought the school lunches were disgusting and wouldn't allow me to eat them. You never noticed how I snuck the cafeteria food in my backpack after I ate what Caiden brought because if I didn't, I wouldn't have had dinner.

Do you remember how you would beg your parents to let me come over? And even though I was dirty and small, and your parents wished you had other friends, you told them that I was yours, and somehow, you got them to listen.

What you didn't know, or you refused to see, was that Caiden also begged your parents just as fiercely, and he also told them that I was his.

I just wanted you to know that if I had known how it all would've ended up, even at eight years old, I would've run as far away from the two of you as I could.

After I turned ten, Dorothy Miller announced to the whole school at lunch that she was going to marry you. So I punched her.

Do you remember that?

For some reason, the cool thing that fall was for everyone to pretend to get married. But you and Caiden were who all the popular girls wanted to marry.

You got jealous because Caiden asked me to marry him first, so you went ahead and pretended to marry Dorothy, even though it made me cry.

Remember showing up at the pretend ceremony during recess? How Caiden stood there looking so serious—well, as serious as an eleven-year-old boy could—and he promised me he was going to love me forever and ever.

You laughed along with the other kids, who laughed because they all knew it was a joke that someone like Caiden would ever really love someone like me.

Remember when you found me crying afterwards, because it was the first time you'd ever laughed at me? Then you started crying because you felt so bad. You told me that even if Caiden loved me, you were going to love me forever and ever, too.

Then you told me you just wanted me to know that you would love me more, no matter what.

And even at ten, I wanted you to kiss me.

When I was twelve, things grew even worse at home. I didn't tell you, because the whole thing was really embarrassing. But you saw bruises on me, and I knew you didn't believe me when I told you I fell down at recess every day playing soccer.

You started walking me home every day after that first time I lied to you. That first day, your parents didn't know where you went, because you hadn't told Caiden, or asked permission. They found us halfway to my house. Your mom was shrieking, because she was so scared. You looked right at her and told her that you had to protect me.

Remember how Caiden got out of the car and hugged me because I was upset that you'd gotten in trouble? Remember how Caiden begged your mom to give me a ride home every day? Remember how she said that she couldn't because she didn't know my mom?

That year was really hard. Maybe all the other years were hard too. But I think what stuck out in my mind about that year was that it was the first time I realized how big the difference between us really was. I had never seen your mom's Range Rover before. I think Mama had sold her car by then to help pay the property taxes on our home.

I told myself in that moment that no matter what, I would keep a small part of myself away from the two of you.

Then you pitched a big fit, and your mom agreed to drop me off that one time, and I realized how hard keeping myself separate from you was going to be.

I was thirteen when Caiden told me you kissed Marcy Thomas. I confronted you and told you that you had ruined everything. I screamed at you about doing it, and you tried to tell me that Marcy was the one that had kissed you. But I didn't care.

We were supposed to be each other's first kiss.

And so when Caiden kissed me under the bleachers a week later...I kissed him back.

It was a fumbling kiss, but still a really good one. And Caiden told me he loved me again, and this time it wasn't because of a fake marriage ceremony. I told him I loved him back, because I did.

But even then, I knew it probably wasn't the same kind of love that he was talking about.

When I got home that night, you don't know this, but I cried. I cried because I wished the whole time that I had been kissing you.

CHAPTER 2

NOW

Beeeeeep. Beeeeeep.

The sound of the hospital equipment ground on my nerves more than usual. Why did I do this to myself? Why did I come every week to sit by the bedside of my former boyfriend? Guilt?

After all, it was my fault he ended up here. It was my fault that the world would never see his wide smile, or the dimple that was only on one cheek.

I thought the guilt would fade in time, release itself the way that sorrow and loss often do. But that hadn't been the case. It had been two years, five months, and eighteen days since I last saw his smile. And even then, the aftermath of what happened that night remained emblazoned in my mind, just as vivid as if it happened yesterday.

The memory of his smile had faded though. All I could remember now was the stark grief on his face now when we last spoke.

He should have been taken off the machine years ago, but his parents hadn't been able to do it. One thing was for certain, you couldn't accuse Caiden's parents of neglect. This room was proof of that, more like a shrine than a hospital bed at this point.

I usually came on Fridays, a punishment of sorts, so I would make sure not to be too happy over the weekend. Which really was stupid, because being "too happy" had never been a threat in my life. I was here on a Monday morning, though, today. It marked a special occasion.

Because in just an hour, I would be starting at a new school, and in just an hour, I would see *him*.

Caiden had always known how to handle Jackson. That brand of darkness inside Jackson, unfathomable to so many, had never frightened Caiden. In a way, they were foils of each other. Fraternal twins and the exact opposites. It always caught people off guard though at how sunny Caiden's disposition had always been. With his black as night hair and even darker brown eyes, he stood in sharp contrast to Jackson's sun god looks.

Maybe his Apollo-like aspect was what threw everyone off about Jackson. Going by his looks alone, he should have been happiness and light personified. So when he went black and savagely punched you in the head and knocked you out because you looked at him wrong...you didn't see it coming.

I fiddled with the blanket on Caiden's bed.

"I think I have to stop coming here," I said softly to his prone form.

For a moment, I almost expected him to answer me.

Of course he didn't. He wouldn't answer me ever again.

At least, that was what the doctors thought. His parents still held out hope for a miracle.

"I think it's time for me to move on," I continued. And it was a relief that he couldn't answer back.

Because what people didn't know about Caiden was that underneath his wide smile was a boy who couldn't let me go.

He called me the loveliest kind of pain.

I called him a monster.

Continue the story at books2read.com/heartbreakprince

JOIN C.R.'S FATED REALM

Visit my **Facebook** page to get updates.

Visit my **Amazon Author** page.

Visit my website at www.crjanebooks.com

Sign up for my **newsletter** to stay updated on new releases, find out random facts about me, and get access to different points of view from my characters.

BOOKS BY C.R. JANE

www.crjanebooks.com

The Sounds of Us Contemporary Series (complete series)

Remember Us This Way

Remember You This Way

Remember Me This Way

Broken Hearts Academy Series: A Bully Romance (complete duet)

Heartbreak Prince

Heartbreak Lover

Ruining Dahlia (Contemporary Mafia Standalone)

Ruining Dahlia

The Fated Wings Series (Paranormal series)

First Impressions

Forgotten Specters

The Fallen One (a Fated Wings Novella)

Forbidden Queens

Frightful Beginnings (a Fated Wings Short Story)

Faded Realms

Faithless Dreams

Fabled Kingdoms

Fated Wings 8

The Rock God (a Fated Wings Novella)

The Darkest Curse Series

Forget Me

Lost Passions

Hades Redemption Series

The Darkest Lover

The Darkest Kingdom

Monster & Me Duet Co-write with Mila Young

Monster's Temptation

Monster's Obsession

Academy of Souls Co-write with Mila Young (complete series)

School of Broken Souls

School of Broken Hearts

School of Broken Dreams

School of Broken Wings

Fallen World Series Co-write with Mila Young (complete series)

Bound

Broken

Betrayed

Belong

Thief of Hearts Co-write with Mila Young (complete series)

Darkest Destiny

Stolen Destiny

Broken Destiny

Sweet Destiny

Kingdom of Wolves Co-write with Mila Young

Wild Moon

Wild Heart

Wild Girl

Wild Love

Wild Soul

Stupid Boys Series Co-write with Rebecca Royce

Stupid Boys

Dumb Girl

Crazy Love

Breathe Me Duet Co-write with Ivy Fox (complete)

Breathe Me

Breathe You

Rich Demons of Darkwood Series Co-write with May Dawson

Make Me Lie

Make Me Beg

Make Me Wild

Printed in Great Britain
by Amazon